THE PEARL
CHRISTMAS ANNUAL

1881

British Library Cataloguing-in-Publication Data
A catalogue record for this book is available from
the British Library

CONTENTS

A HISTORY OF EROTIC LITERATURE

Erotic literature today is associated with *Fifty Shades of Grey* or internet pornography, but erotic fiction has existed for centuries. Erotic literature comes in many forms, including novels, poems, memoirs, such as Casanova's *Histoire de ma Vie* (1822) and manuals, such as the *Kama Sutra*. It covers a range of taboo subjects such as sadomasochism, homosexuality and prostitution whilst often being satirical and socially critical. Erotic literature is loosely defined as fictional and factual accounts of human sexual relationships which have the power to or are intended to arouse the reader sexually, indicating why the genre has historically been so controversial.

Erotic literature was not considered a huge problem before the invention of the printing press because, due to the costs of producing individual manuscripts, there was a limited readership. Early erotic poetry in Ancient Greece by Sappho of Lesbos, or Ovid for example, was only read by a select few. During the Renaissance, erotic poetry, such as Shakespeare's sonnets, often circulated as a manuscript and therefore had a limited readership. That is not to imply that people never had a problem with erotica. Giovanni Boccaccio's *Decameron* (1353) depicted the lechery of monks and the seclusion of nuns and was banned in many countries. Erotic literature was often censored and destroyed on the grounds of obscenity and was mainly criticised by the ecclesiastical courts. In England, after the Reformation, the church lost much of its power to the Crown which licensed every published book and prosecutions of books for their erotic content were rare.

The first conviction for obscenity in England was in 1727 when Edmund Curll was fined for disturbing the King's peace with his work, *The Venus in the Cloister, or The Nun in Her Smock*. This set the precedent for other legal convictions. Prosecutions in the later eighteenth century were rare and often related to mixing seditious and blasphemous material. John Wilkes' and Thomas Potter's *An Essay on Woman* (1763), based on Alexander Pope's *An Essay on Man* (1733-34), featured parodies on Pope's work, such as *A Dying Lover to his Prick* (based on Pope's *A Dying Christian to his Soul*). The work was the only erotic work to ever be read out in full in the House of Lords before being declared obscene and Wilkes being deemed an outlaw. The Obscene Publications Act (1857) made the sale of obscene material a statutory offence and gave the courts the power to seize and destroy offending material, but it did not define the obscene. Therefore, the work affected by it changed. The Act was originally against works that were written to corrupt others and focused on overt erotica, but this changed and the focus moved onto works which affected someone who was open to corruption, rather than focusing on the writer's intent. It led to many high profile seizures and the targeting of renowned classics by authors such as D.H. Lawrence, James Joyce and medical textbooks by Havelock Ellis. The Act changed again in the 1950s to focus on pure pornography.

Despite its torrid legal history, erotic literature has a diverse past with a huge authorship. In the seventeenth century John Wilmot, Earl of Rochester (1647-1680) was notorious for his obscene verses. His reputation as a libertine meant that his name was often used as a selling point by publishers of collections of erotic verse. Michel Millot's and Jean L'Ange's *L'Ecole des Filles* (1655) concerned the sexual education of younger naïve women, by an older, experienced woman which was a popular theme in erotic literature. The novel was hugely popular and was even mentioned in Samuel Pepys diary where, in an often censored passage, he records masturbating over the work. A unique work during this period was *Sodom, or the Quintessence of Debauchery* (1684), a closet play by John Wilmot 2nd Earl of Rochester, which focused on buggery and homosexuality. Edmund Curll's

Merryland books were also a peculiar version of English erotic fiction where the female body (and sometimes male form) were described in terms of a landscape. The rise of the novel in the eighteenth century gave writers a new platform for erotic literature. John Cleland's *Fanny Hill* (1748) set a high standard for literary smut. This period was a high point for English erotica, after which it declined in the 1750s with the introduction of romanticism, however the genre stayed popular in Europe. One French genre was influenced by the translation of *Arabian Nights* and involved the transformation of people into various objects which were then used in sexual relationships. Denis Diderot's *Les Bijoux Indiscrets* (1747) tells of a magic ring which is used to get women's vaginas to reveal their intimate sexual histories. In the late eighteenth century, novels such as *120 Days of Sodom* (1785) by Marquis de Sade, from whom sadism is derived, explored sadomasochism and influenced sadist and masochistic novels later in the genre.

Victorian erotica was often written by hacks, but interestingly featured curious forms of social stratification. Social distinctions between a master and his servant were never forgotten or ignored, even during sex. There were also often significant examples of sadomasochism, perhaps due to the public school culture and the emphasis on flagellation as a form of corporeal punishment. Novels were often written under pseudonyms or anonymously, for example *The Lustful Turk* (1828) by Rosa Coote. Erotic poets included George Colman the Younger and Algernon Charles Swinburne who wrote twelve eclogues on flagellation. There was also a rise in clandestine erotic periodicals, such as *The Pearl* which contained collections of erotic tales, songs and parodies. Another important European erotic work was *Venus in Furs* (1870) by Leopold von Sacher-Masoch. He brought the world's attention to masochism and this fetish was named after him.

Towards the end of the nineteenth century erotic literature became more cultured and was associated with the Decadent Movement, of which Aubrey Beardsley's *Yellow Book* (1894-

97) was an influential work. There was also a rise in pioneering homosexual novels, such as *The Sins of the Cities of the Plain* (1881) and *Teleny or the Reverse of the Medal* (1893). Erotic literature remained prolific well into the twentieth century and included works, such as *Alter of Venus* (1934), Henry Miller's *Tropic of Cancer* (1934), Paulina Rénage's *Story of O* (1954) and Anais Nin's *Delta of Venus* (1978). It has continued in its popularity and diversity since then and remains a popular genre within modern day society.

NEW YEAR'S DAY;
THE
TO
SWILIA

CHAPTER I

Le Jour de l'An.

PAST FOUR O'CLOCK IN THE AFTERNOON, AND I'm only just out of bed; how I have slept since that little devil of a Fuckatilla left me at 7 a.m.! Well, I must dress and make up as if just arrived so as to deceive the old mother, it won't do for her to 6nd out I've slept with the pretty Susan all night. Ha, what a clever little schemer she is to suggest that she would sleep in my bed to air it against the morrow, when I was to return to town, and then let me know so I could let myself in after the old woman was gone to bed. By Jove! I think it is well aired now, we've been fucking in it like steam, spending the old year out and the new year in; I believe our first fuck ended in a delightful spend on both sides just as Big Ben struck twelve. Now I'll make haste, then ring for Mrs. Childings, and order the supper; what a happy thought that of mine, promising to send her down to my aunt's at Richmond, as soon as I got back, she will stay there all night, and

Fuckatilla will fetch her cousin to help, the same as on Christmas Eve, that ever-to-be-re-membered Christmas Eve, it beats all the fun I ever had, but my name's not Priapus Bigcock if we don't top it tonight.

At last he left the bedroom in great coat and hat, with a small valise, as if just arrived from a journey, closed the door behind him, and rang the bell for the housekeeper.

"Mrs. Childings, a Happy New Year to you, didn't expect me quite so soon, I must have a fire at once if you will be so good as to send Susan up to light it," he said, Ringing aside his overcoat and taking off his wrapping. "I've had a fine bracing journey up to town, its a lovely day to begin the year with; by-the-bye can you run down at once to my aunt's at Richmond, her cook is ill, and they have a party coming on this evening. I would have stopped myself, but for my previous engagement with my old chums this evening. I promised you should start at once, so Susan shall fetch her cousin to do for us as soon as she has lighted the fire. Make haste, aunt is in a terrible muddle, it will be two guineas in your pocket, and I knew you could help her better than any one; those confectioners and other fellows she is obliged to employ, worry her to death, and you can take all that off her hands. Never mind about us, we can be jolly and how, start off quick."

Too pleased with her job, Mrs. Childings quickly thanked him for recommending her, and left the room to send up Susan, and start off herself.

"My little darling!" exclaimed the Hon. Priapus, coming behind the pretty girl as soon as she had entered and was kneeling in front of the empty grate, "haven't I arranged it all finely, make haste and fetch Emma," as he caught up her clothes behind and exposed her splendid bottom, just peeping out between the open slit of her pretty drawers; the sight makes him randy in a moment, his big prick is out, and ready for a fuck dog fashion, in spite of Fuckatilla's protestations for him to be quiet, and keep his nonsense till the evening, "I'll burn it with the poker if you don't leave me alone, you impudent fellow!"

"Ha, I like that idea, especially as you have to light the fire and warm it first, I'll poker you; my prick doesn't want a fire to warm it, it's boiling over already!" he laughed, not able to retain himself from spending all over her bottom, the playful resistance of the girl had so excited him.

"What a shame!" she said, "to go on so, no one would think how you had indulged with me all last night, and now to begin again so soon, sir," as she put her hand behind and guided the shaft of love to her longing slit. "See, you can't get in unless I let you, you naughty, bad boy!"

"But now I'm in I guess I'll stop there as the dog said," he laughed, clasping her firmly round the buttocks and fucking away furiously. "How deliciously tight it feels this way, I can quite fancy its your little gas pipe behind that is nipping my prick so beautifully."

"Push, push, fuck, fuck," she almost screamed in reply, "this is the finest way we have found out yet, you seem to get so far in, and to excite me more than ever. Oh, oh, oh! I'm coming, I can't stop it!" as she really fainted away in delight, and nearly unshipped his cock at the moment of spending, by going Rat on the hearthrug, where she lay whilst he revelled in the tightness and voluptuous contractions of her vagina.

At length he withdrew his dripping tool, and turned his attention to the girl, who speedily came round when he sprinkled her face with cold water, opening her eyes with a loving smile on her lips as she slowly realized who it was attending to her.

"How heavenly! how delightful!" she sighed.

"I seem to have enjoyed an age of bliss, how long did I faint?"

"Not five minutes, my little dear," he replied. "Now we will be serious, and behave ourselves till Frank Jones arrives; he's sure to be first again. Light the fire, and then fetch your cousin Emma at once, and do you know another nice little girl you could get to stop all night with you, and join in our games?"

Fuckatilla rather pouted at this suggestion, but her pretty face speedily relaxed again into a smile, as she said, "So you want a change, do you? I'll serve you out for it when you least expect it, sir! Wasn't I enough for you last night, and equal to all your lecherous ideas?"

"Just listen to the jealous hussey, she wants my cock all to herself!" laughed the young barrister. "You shall have a prick in your cunt, arse, mouth, and hand all at once before tomorrow morning, if you only get us another nice little girl as pretty as yourself, my dear, try your best and you'll get a fine New Year's gift."

"Little Nell is just the girl for you," replied Fuckatilla. "Nothing delights her so much as to see cats, dogs, or rabbits fucking, although she's not quite thirteen, and I'm sure doesn't know what it is herself; besides, she's such a delicicus little titbit, I've often tickled her myself for fun; we call her Nelly Raquet because she was found on a doorstep in Racquet Court, by an old printer, who having no children of

his own, took the pretty baby home, and kept her as a daughter ever since, but she's a perfect little devil for fun, and sure not to split, whatever we may let her see or join in."

"All right, dear Fuckatilla, only mind, jealousy's a thing we don't admit here. You girls must be all love and no selfishness, then everything will be charming," replied the voluptuous minded young roue as he hummed —

The ladies, the ladies, I love them all, So let them be stout, or let them be thin,

Or let them be short, or let them be tall, My prick's so randy I'm sure to get in;

I've a fuck, a fuck, a fuck for them all!

them's my sentiments, my love!"

"Very well, sir, I'm sure you are virtue itself in disguise," replied the lively girl, "but let me advise you to take a walk on the Embankment or somewhere for a couple of hours, and leave all the arrangements to me, and cousin Emma. She will be here presently, as I guessed your little game and asked her to come by five o'clock."

Returning from his stroll about half-past seven, the Hon. Priapus as he ascended the staircase to his chambers, was astonished at hearing the voice of his friend Frank Jones threatening somebody if they would not do something; so he proceeded cautiously on tip-toe to learn what fun was up, and listening at the key-hole heard him say, "The impudent little thing, doesn't mind handling or stroking my prick, but won't suck it, well see about that, won't we Fuckatilla? Now, just take her across your lap; that's it, turn up her skirts, let us have a good look at her pretty bum. Ha, I must kiss it, wait a moment before you begin to slap."

Just at this instant his Hon. friend thought of a famous peep-hole he had once made in the wall for some purpose, so shifting his position, he was soon in full view of the parties inside his room. It was indeed a sight to give any one a rampant cockstand. There was Fuckatilla holding the struggling little Nelly Raquet across her knees as she sat on the sofa, whilst Frank Jones was helping her lift the girl's petticoats, Consin Emma was by the side of Frank, who had his breeches down, and his prick at full cock, which she was frigging beautifully, pulling back the foreskin from its ruby head at every motion of her hand, whilst her eyes seemed beaming with sensual desires as she regarded the object of her caresses.

"Hold the little devil, or she will kick my face!" exclaimed Frank, kneeling down and shoving his nose between the cheeks of the little girl's bottom, where no doubt his tongue was busy tickling the virgin slit." "Ha!" he exclaimed, "you see I will kiss your cunney for you, Miss Nelly, now won't you promise to kiss my little cockey?"

"Ah! No, never!" was the sharp response of the little girl, "the nasty thing would be sick in my mouth. It was, you know, all over my hands as I was stroking it."

"You won't!" said Frank, getting up and turning to Emma, who he pulled on his lap, "Then Fuckatilla shall slap your bum, till you promise to give it a good suck, not only a kiss, mind!"

13

"No, I'll never do such a nasty trick. Ah! oh! oh! you hurt so! What a shame!" she screamed, as the smart painful slaps began to tingle her bottom.

"Go on! go on! Don't spare the obstinate little hussey!" exclaimed Frank, "it's delicious to see her kicking, and watch the constant shifting of the rosy Rush on her delicate white flesh at each impact of your hand on her tight skinned rump."

He had now got Emma fairly astraddle across his lap as he sat on a chair where she was riding him impetuously *a la St. George*, with her petticoats well up, so that the action of her bottom could be seen beautifully, in fact Frank's hands being round her waist under her clothes, kept them so, and he has pulled her drawers well open, so that he could see everything in the glass over the mantle-piece, which divided his attention with the interesting slapping match going on upon the sofa.

But it was the latter scene which most interested the gentleman at the peep-hole. Nelly Raquet was such a piquant little beauty, though not quite thirteen, she was small for her age, but beautifully formed, her feet, legs and bottom, were as exquisitely shaped as any Epicurean could wish to feast his eyes upon, whilst her face, which he could see perfectly, although it was turned away from Frank, had its beauty heightened by the crimson blushes of shame by which it was suffused, at being so humiliated before a gentleman; large dark flashing eyes, in which the tears sparkled like diamonds, and a set of pearly teeth, rosy lips, and black glossy hair as fine as silk made a *tout ensemble*, sufficiently ravishing to whet the appetite of a rone, however satiated he might have felt before she met his view.

"By jingo!" exclaimed Mr. Priapus Bigcock *sotto voce*, "she's a dainty bit that would stir up my blood had I been as old and effete as Beaconsfield himself, by-the-bye, I wonder if champagne jelly is good to induce sensual desires in old people, I'll ask my uncle to try it; he told me last night he hadn't had a rise since he was made a judge six years ago, it's a pity such a jolly old cockolorum can't enjoy a bit of young cunt now and then."

Meanwhile the game inside was progressing rapidly.

Frank and Emma seemed to come together in a luscious spend, whilst Fuckatilla, to judge by her excited loks, was also spending from the effects of sympathy, and the sight of the pretty wriggling bottom, she was so artistically slapping, for presently her hand dropped upon the rosy bum of her little victim, and slipping down to her cunney, tickled the darling with her fingers, till Bigcock could see the glistening of spendings on them as they worked in and out of the tight little sheath. Nelly turned up her face to Fucktilla, her eyes beaming with love and excitement as she clasped her friend round the neck with both arms, and kissed her rapturously, as she said with an agitated voice, "How my bum burns, and enjoys the tickling of your fingers, dear, it's so delicious I would do anything to feel like that again!"

She was now told to kiss Mr. Jone's cock quickly or Mr. Bigcock would catch them there, and whip them all unmercifully with a big birch rod, "And that, my dear, you would and no laughing matter, when it cuts your flesh till the blood comes!"

Here Bigcock, who had spent in his breeches, thought it time to put a stop to further proceedings, or it would spoil Jones and the girls for fun after supper, so suddenly opening the door, he frightened poor little Nelly almost out of her wits, by exclaiming, "So I will, I'm really astonished at Mr. Jones behaving so with you girls. It's most disgusting, you shall all be well whipped before twelve o'clock, or my name's not what it is; be off, you two, (turning to the other girls), leave Nelly with me, or she may run home, and make haste to have the supper ready!"

Fuckatilla and Emma vanished at once with a sly glance of fun at Mr. Priapus, as he took the alarmed Nelly on his lap. The door being closed, he went on to question his friend Frank, as to his early arrival.

"The fact is, old fellow," replied Jones, "that I have been quite demoralized by your Christmas Eve's entertainment, the delights of that night are ever running through my brain, and last night again I had another wonderful dream, such scenes, and such reality about it all."

"So much the better, my boy, said Bigcock, "it will be something to relate after supper, but how about being here so early, nine o'clock was the time you know?"

"I longed so to see the girls again, my cock has been standing all day at the thoughts of it, that at last, in a fit of desperation, I started too soon, hoping to enjoy a smoke with you, but as luck would have it, I dropped upon these three dear girls having a frig and gamahuche on the sofa, as I entered without knocking, the door not being properly closed," said Jones.

"Well, go on, teil me ail about it."

"You see, Nelly here, was kissing Fuckatilla's fanny," he continued, "whilst Cousin Emma had got a dildoe, or something, to fuck herself with; I suppose they found it in one of your drawers, it was only a few minutes before you burst in upon us. My first impulse was to withdraw."

"Tell that to the marines, Frank," interrupted his friend. "If your cock didn't stand in a moment I'll forfeit a pony, and call up the girls to decide!"

Never mind about betting, I might lose," continued Frank with a laugh, as he could see that Bigcock had his hand under the little girl's clothes, as she sat on his knee with her face hidden in his bosom. "Emma sprang towards me at once, exclaiming, 'A man, a man, just the thing we want, and had my breeches unbuttoned in a moment, searched for and drew out my stiff prick before the astonished Nelly, asking her if she would not like to stroke such a fine plaything. Nelly was bashful but not timid, although she blushed up to her eyes; they made hep handle and stroke my prick up and down, but the little dear would not look in my face, her eyes were all for Mr. Jones's big thing, which presently astonished her by being what she called sick over her hands, and would not touch it again. The girls were too excited, but I heard you come up to the door, and once or twice heard a sigh or a grunt as the scene affected you, so no doubt you know all the rest."

"Just so," replied the Hon. Priapus. "Now, Nelly Racquet, that's your name, I believe, you must give me a kiss."

The girl looked up, her fine large eyes suffused with tears, whilst her lovely face was almost of a damask hue, overspread as it was with blushes of shame at hearing Frank tell everything she had done.

"Don't be shamefaced, or frightened Nelly, we like you too much, and will show you such fun; now didn't you like Fuckatilla's finger tickling your cunney after the slapping. I could see how you hugged and kissed her?" taking the girl's lovely blushing face between both his hands and holding it up for a kiss almost sucking her breath away.

"It's all so new, I'm afraid," sighed the little girl.

"Afraid of what my dear? Is it this?" as he let out his great fiery-headed battering ram, and placed it in her hand; "It's the most tender-hearted thing in the world, and was made for little girls to play with."

"La, sir! that's what makes the babies, a big girl told me so one day. I was looking at some dogs, as cruel boys were beating them with sticks to separate them; she said a man's thing was exactly like a dog's in shape, but I'm not afraid, sir. It can't hurt me, I'm so young. Do men and women stick together like dogs?" asked the sophisticated girl.

"That's right, stroke it up and down," said the barrister, "but why do you ask such a question?" as he was now tickling and gently frigging her tight little cunt again, and kissing her all the while.

"Because a big boy once wanted me to let him do it to me, but I wouldn't, though I let him feel and tickle me as you do, and I played with his cockey. I was afraid we might stick together and get caught," she replied.

Here Frank Jones was so excited that he declared Bigcock was not to have all the fun to himself, and with his breeches still down, presented his stiff prick for her to caress.

Nelly took one in each hand, blushing deeply again, yet with a loving smile as she looked in their excited faces, "What impudent things!" she exclaimed, as she seemed to tremble all over, "shall I rub their noses together? You know girls play at flatcock, haven't you boys ever done anything of the sort together?"

"Yes, yes! that's delightful, you little dear; pull the skins back and rub the heads together!" gasped both of them almost simultaneously as they both spent at once, and the sperm dripped from between her fingers as she held the two throbbing heads of their penises tightly together.

Each kissed her rapturously, almost knocking their heads together, in their hurry to do so, then when a little calmer, Bigcock and Jones put their affairs out of sight, after making Nelly first wipe them with a soft towel and kiss each cockey, and tickle the tip of the eurethra with her tongue for a moment, just to prove her love. The former now opened a drawer, and pulling out a very pretty young lady's watch and chain, presented them to the astonished and grateful girl.

The presentation was hardly over before Spencer and Jack Turdey arrived. The latter at once perceived that he had been too late for some of the fun, as he observed whilst shaking hands with his friends, "You might have asked me to come a little earlier, but I'll have a kiss of this delicious little child before I enquire more!" kissing Nelly very amorously on her cherry lips. "It's no slight, I can assure you my old chum; you can see something has happened, but it was solely owing to circumstances over which we had no control," said Bigcock, "I had even got this precious little darling as an extra treat for our after supper seance of love."

"Ah! Ha! ha! ! that's good, is it not Spencer? So I suppose the circumstances over which you had no control were your randy pricks, the sight of her was too much for you, eh," laughed Jack.

"Only a feel, and a spend or two; she's a real little virgin," said Frank deprecatingly.

"Well," replied Jack, "you fellows deserve birching or bottom fucking for it, that's all I have to say. I'm not jealous, only devilishly inclined for a fuctious evening."

No more was said about it, but their host observing that supper would be ready in a few minutes, asked if they had heard the new anecdote about the Prince of Wales' visit to the East London Hospital?

"No, old fellow, let's have it"

"It's not much," continued the host, "His Royal Highness went to inspect the East London Hospital, so going into the male-ward, he asked the man in No. 1 bed, "What's the matter with you my man, are you comfortable, or have you any complaints?"

PATIENT.—Got the pox, your Royal Highness, the doctors do all they can for me, and the nurses are very kind, everything's so nice, I shall be sorry to go out again when I am well, because I'm a very poor man.

H.R.H.—Noble institution, glad to hear you are so well cared for. Goes on to No. 2 bed, "Well, my man, how are you, what's the matter with you?"

PATIENT.—Pretty well, your Royal Highness, got a bad fistula, but everything's nice and everybody is kind to me.

H.R.H.—Beautiful charity, quite a paradise for the sick poor to come to; and what may be the matter with you? addressing the man in No. 3 bed.

PATIENT.—Got an ulcer in my mouth, obliged to have my jaws tied up, your Royal Highness, in a very sepulchral voice.

H.R.H.—Well, how are you getting on?

PATIENT.—-Only pretty well, your Royal Highness.

H.R.H.-—-Only pretty well, have you got any complaint to make?

PATIENT.—-Yes, your Royal Highness, I want to go into No. 1 bed. I want to see the doctor first!

H.R.H.—What's that for, don't you have proper attention?

PATIENT.—Well your Royal Highness, the doctor goes to that fellow in No. 1 bed and pulls his cock about, then he goes to No. 2, and shoves his finger up his arse, and then he comes and puts his finger in my mouth; I want to see the doctor first.

H.R.H.—Very reasonable, shouldn't like that myself; I'll make a note of it, and then *sotto voce*, filthy places these hospitals after all, I pity the poor beggars who get into them, they may have to eat shit or pox juice, or what not; I don't think I'll go much further round, I've a most pressing engagement.

CHAPTER II

Frank Jones' dream of the Sack of London
by the Germans after the Battle of Dorking.

Supper was now announced, but it is needless to say much about that, except that the four young gentlemen again treated all the girls as if they were perfect ladies. Nelly Racquet was a great favourite, but her two friends were not in the least jealous of the constant attention of the Hon. Priapus and his chums, to their younger companion, who delighted her new found acquaintances by the display of ready and pert replies to all their sallies and badinage.

"Jack," said the barrister to his friend, "what do you think? Our little Nelly here was telling us that a big boy once proposed to her to let him do as the dogs do, only she was afraid they might stick together, but you played with his little cock, didn't you, my dear?"

"Oh, yes! I wasn't afraid to do that, you should have seen how he pushed it in and out of my hand, and his red face and startling eyes, as he almost screamed, 'Oh ! ! oh ! ! oh ! ! ! it's coming, it's coming, Nelly,' and then the thick cream drops spurted out. It was the first time I had ever seen anything of the sort, and was afraid I had hurt him."

SPENCER.—She's a sly little thing. I'll warrant you a good whipping if you don't tell us all he did to you!

NELLY.—That was all at that time, except his tickling my little pussey, as he called it, with his finger.

JACK.—What do yo umean by "at that time," did he do anything else another day?

NELLY.—I really can't tell you any more, I should be so ashamed, blushing furiously as she thought of what she had allowed the boy to do.

They all saw that there was something behind the blush and supper being over they determined to hear what it was.

"Now," said Jack, "we must know what it was that you did that time; it must have been something 6ne, or you would never blush so."

NELLY.—I'll never tell, indeed I won't.

SPENCER.—Then we must try a light stinging switch; Jack, will you lay her over your lap, and turn up her clothes as artistically as possible.

Nelly, who had up to this, been rather impudently de6ant, was seized and drawn across the lap of Jack Rurdey, in spite of her screams and protestations, her quivering lips and tearful eyes only adding to the enjoyment of the company, who began to get quite excited as the pretty fat buttocks were gradually exposed to view.

"Ah! no!! no!!!" she screamed. "I can't stand that again. Mr. Jones slapped me so before, my poor bum is quite sore!"

"Just what I expected, you and Bigcock had been up to," said Jack, and then sternly to Nellie. "I want to know all about that boy, not about my friends here; there, will that make you speak out?" giving a sharp slap with his heavy hand, which sounded clearly through the room, leaving an intermixture of white and rosy marks on the poor girl's smarting bum, where his hand fell. "Do you want another, my little dear, to make you tell us?" smacking her again still harder, regardless of her cries and kicks, which quite delighted them all.

"Wait stop!! Ah, no more, pray sir!" sobbed the beautiful little victim, the tears running down her crimson cheeks, "I will, I will tell you all!"

"Then sit up on my knee and speak out, you dear little silly, so that we can all hear," said Jack, lifting her up, but keeping her clothes up by one arm round her waist, as he kissed the tearful face, and kept his other hand in possession of her unfledged cunney, "I didn't want to hurt you, but we must know all about it."

"Well, you must know," she began, "it is not long ago, but one day he found out I was all alone in the house, so that bad, rude Charlie knocked at the door, and rushed in soon as it was opened, dragged me into the little parlour, threw me down, and began what he called a rare lark, but I assure you it was no fun to me, he turned up my clothes, slapped my rump so that I screamed with pain, and then turning me over on my back, he spit on my pussey, and said it was a silly looking thing without hair on it, so he painted it all round with a bit of coal; you can't tell how ashamed and angry I was with him for being so rough and nasty. I struggled and tried to bite him, but he was so strong I lost all my strength, and lay sobbing and crying on the hearth-rug; then the beast declared he would serve me still worse, but — but — but I can't tell any more; oh pray don't ask me!"

"Go on," said Jack, sternly, "or we shall serve you still worse. Did he shove his cock into you here?" tickling her cunney with his forefinger.

"Oh, no, worse and worse," sobbed the ashamed girl, "but I can't tell!"

"Well, then," said Jack, "I guess it was there, was it not?" as he was trying to push his forefinger up Nelly's little tight fundament.

"Ah! Oh, no! Never again!" screamed the prisoner. "It hurts so, and is so nasty."

"I thought we should find out," said Jack, delighted at his success. "So he got in there, did he?"

"Oh, it was cruel," sobbed Nelly. "He thumped me about so because I kept the cheeks of my bottom tightly together; he had turned me on my face, you must know, and at last when I was nearly dead, he got a lump of butter off the table and greased the hole, then forced his stiff cock right up my behind. Now pray let me go, sir!"

"But that wasn't all, besides Emma here knows all about it, so we will birch you dreadfully, if you don't say how he finished with you!" exclaimed Spencer, who was being gently frigged by the cousin.

Too frightened to refuse she continued to relate how Charlie seemed to spurt something warm into her, and that when he drew his affair out, it was followed by a small quantity of excrement, as she could not help herself, which so enraged him that he wiped his soiled cock on her face, and tried to shove it into her mouth. "Now," she concluded, "I have really told you everything, and he would have been locked up, only I was too ashamed to go against him; I only wish I could serve him out, as he always laughs when he meets me, and smacks his lips as if tasting something nice."

This tale had so worked them all up that Jack now called Nelly's attention to what the others were doing, as she had been hiding her blushing tearful face on his bosom as his fingers frigged her tight bum-hole and cunney both at once, whilst she had stammered out the account of Charlie's outrageous conduct.

Cousin Emma was riding on Spencer's pego, which could be seen going in and out of her lecherous gap, as she sat astride of his lap, and rode up and down on his shaft, her lips glued to his, and her tongue in Ms mouth. Each time she went up the vermillion lips of her cunt could be seen protruding as they seemed to cling tightly round . the rather brown looking cock they were sucking so deliciously, and which glistened with their mutual spendings.

The Hon. Priapus was seated on the sofa with Fuckatilla on his lap, his 6ne large instrument buried to the roots of its hair in her beautiful cunt, she had her back to him but his arms were keeping up her clothes, and his hands tickling her slit in front through the opening of her drawers. Frank Jones stood close in front of the amorous girl, who had her hands on his pego, ticking his balls and caressing the shaft, exposing the bursting head of his jewel at every backward motion of her hand, as she softly passed it up and down. The scene was exquisite, Jack hugged his trembling little partner to Ms bosom, and afraid to attempt her ravishment at the moment, placed his throbbing prick in her hand, and whispered in her ear to place it between her thighs, and close them tightly upon it, whilst he reclined backwards, and held her between his legs, making her ride on his affair with her toes just touching the floor; thus he had all the sensations of a delicious fuck without hurting little Nelly; each one seemed to try to prolong the pleasure, but although their movements were . very slow and gentle, the sight of each other's enjoyment had such a stimulating effect that they all seemed to come at the same moment, Jack's spending's flying out a good distance on the floor, from between the cheeks of Nelly's buttocks, just as the others all died away in extasy.

"Now for full dress, 'beauty unadorned,'" said the host, "or we shall be too warm to appreciate Frank's new dream, I only hope it is as good as the last, about the circus performance."

They were soon divested of every covering, and after a glass of champagne all round, Frank was ready to relate how he dreamt the old year out, and the new year in, so taking Cousin Emma on his lap, he made her keep a. hand on his now limp concern, whilst he had two of his Angers groping about her clitoris.

"When I went to bed last night," he began, "I really meant to lay awake and hear all the church bells join in their annual welcome to the new year, but it generally happens that we sleep when we want to keep our eyes open, and vice versa; just so with me, I couldn't keep awake for the life of me, and was presently dreaming all sorts of rubbish; during the day I had casually looked into that old pamphlet about the defeat of the English by the Germans at the battle of Dorking, so I suppose my dream turned that way, for I seemed to be in my studio, when old Lord Dufferstones rushed in almost frantic with fear, exclaiming, 'Jones, what awful news, the army is beaten and the guards annihilated, the Germans will sack London and ravish our wives and daughters as soon as they can get here!"

"Every man must fight for his home, I'll do my best to kill at least one enemy before they do for me, and let everyone else do the same, and the bloodthirsty rascals will find it costs them dear," I replied, feeling quite a hero in the presence of the old coward.

" 'Oh, dear! oh, dear! it's no use, Jones, we shall all be slaughtered like sheep!' he raved, tearing his hair.

"Without waiting to hear any more from him I seized a sword and a revolver, and rushed out into the Strand, where I soon heard that the Uhlans had already reached Steatham, and were also close to New Cross in another direction.

"Night was coming on, there were dense crowds in the streets some armed, others clamouring for arms, each one encouraging the other to fight to the last. A perfect panic prevailed at the Northern and Eastern Railway Stations, especially as all the trains went away loaded with fugitive women and children, and none but old men were allowed to accompany them, but it soon came to an end for the want of rolling stock, as the companies having once got it away, would not let any empties return for more, lest the enemy might capture them.

"All night we worked away, making barricades on Westminster Bridge, supported by others in Parliament Street, a few old officers directing the workers, but no general plan of defence seemed to be carried out, as there was no general anywhere, they had all gone out with the army, and had been killed, captured, or prevented from retreating on the capital.

"At last morning came, and we could soon hear the sound of distant firing, which gradually came nearer and nearer, till the attack was commenced on all the bridges at once, from London bridge to Putney.

"Without artillery it was impossible to stem the advancing tide of Germans, they carried the bridges very quickly, shooting and bayonetting the defenders in thousands; now they surged into the bottom of Parliament Street, and as I sat on one of the bronze lions at the foot of the Nelson column encouraging everyone to die rather than yield, I could see the battle slowly coming up to the Horse Guards, and also that the Houses of Parliament were on Are.

Waterloo Bridge was gone, and the enemy now began to take us in Hank from the Strand, whilst others having passed Vauxhall were already swarming the parks and Belgravia, and in possession of Buckingham Palace.

What could an undisciplined rabble do against such a converging host of trained soldiers. The English mob kept up a weak and almost useless fire, and only stood to be slaughtered; I reserved the shots in my revolver till sure of my men, and had the luck to shoot two Germans, then the surging mass carried me away into Pall Mall, where I stumbled over a dead body, and was getting up again when a fierce looking German officer tried to finish me off with his sword, but I shot him dead, and a sudden idea Hashing across my mind, as the surging combatants left me free for a moment. I drew his body inside the doorway of a house which seemed to be deserted, then shutting the door, I stripped off his clothes, and in a very few minutes had so dressed myself in his uniform that anyone would have taken me for a German, now, thought I to myself, I speak German like a native, so as resistance is no longer possible, I will join the enemy in sacking and looting my own native city, so as to see what it is like.

"When I emerged I had smeared my face with blood, and my uniform was also bloodstained. The street was full of corpses, all English, except a single German here and there. A fresh regiment of the enemy was just hurrying past, eager to get to the front, or join in the loot, to judge by their excited faces. Seeing, as he thought, a wounded compatriot, an officer offered me his brandy flask, asking if I was much hurt. The draught gave me fresh courage, and I assured him it was nothing serious, but that I had no doubt been struck down and left for dead, but had recovered myself, and now felt able to join the fight again.

"'We're ordered to occupy Belgrave Square, and prevent the

houses being plundered,' he replied, 'but it will be rare fun, the fellows can't be restrained, none of us have had a woman for a month, we shall ravish them first, and protect the women afterwards. The English dogs would serve us the same if they had the chance. Come along with us, my father is our colonel, and a rare old boy to enjoy himself in war time!'

"What sights I saw as I went along, numbers of straggling soldiers were already plundering everywhere; at the bottom of St. James' Street three of them had got so many pretty girls tied back to back to a lamp-post, with scarcely a rag to cover them, and were fucking them furiously, their blood-stained pricks showing how the poor girls had been ravished, their shrieks and cries were awful, whilst I shall never forget the shame, horror, and humiliation depicted on their countenances.

"'That's a fine sight, my boys!' shouted our old grey-headed colonel, 'let's make haste to our billet, we shall find real ladies there to amuse ourselves with.'

"The men and officers all cheered, and we went on at the double quick, taking no notice of the horrible scenes and carnage through which we passed, and at last we reached our destination, and as luck would have it, the very first house attacked belonged to old Dufferstones. Our colonel, with his son and several other officers, established themselves in the drawing rooms, where they found a profusion of wine and refreshments set out as if for expected guests.

"'I'll wager there's ladies not far off, no men would have had the sense to make such provision for enemies; have the house thoroughly searched, and bring our hostesses here as soon as possible!' ordered the chief with a chuckle of delight, 'Mein Gott fur Kaiser und Vaterland,' as he drained his glass of champagne, and began to attack a fine game pie. 'Look sharp all, so as to be ready for the ladies when they're found, my old prick wants something extra piquante to excite him.'

"All the while we could still hear the infernal din of distant fighting, gradually receding in the distance, but presently we

27

heard several piercing shrieks, evidently from the cellars of the mansion, and very soon an old sergeant announced to the colonel that they had secured three beautiful young ladies, besides several female servants.

"'Very well, bring the ladies here, and keep the other women for yourselves down below, but be gentle, if only done properly no end of men can hurt a girl,' replied the colonel, then turning to me, 'Ah, sir, you're a stranger, so I will just tell you an amusing thing that occurred when the regiment I was quartered at a country village in Pomerania not long ago.'

'Well, a lot of our boys attended the annual fair, and got hold of one of the wenches, everyone enjoying her in turn till they let her go.'

"'You would have thought she would have complained of the outrage, but nothing of the kind. Her brother hearing of it in some way, at once taxed her with having had nineteen soldiers at the fair. "So I did," she replied, "and what do you think my affair got so excited at their coming on one after the other that the lips of my cunt were as stiff as the rim of that saucepan on the fire; it was delightful, I didn't mind it, and will have them again some day, so you just keep to your own business."

"Here the sergeant, who had been respectfully waiting till his superior had finished, informed us that they had found an old gentleman, evidently the father of the English ladies.

" 'Tie his hands behind his back, and bring him with his daughters, and sergeant, see if you can make two or three good flogging instruments out of anything you can find in the house,' were the orders he received.

"We had not long to wait before the soldiers brought in the captives, three beautiful girls and the old man, who I at once recognised as Lord Dufferstones and Ladies Nora, Kathleen, and Ellen Dufferstones, his idolized daughters, none of them seemed to recognise me.

"The colonel, in excellent English, at once enquired of his lordship who they were.

"Lord Dufferstones, his face as white as his gray hair, and in a dreadful fright, great drops of perspiration could be seen hanging in beads on his forehead, or trickling down his grimy face (he had been found in a coal cellar). 'Have mercy, Excellency, I'm a non-combatant, and the dear girls are my loved children, you can have any ransom you like to demand for our safety and protection.'

" 'Indeed,' replied the chief, 'you English are awfully rich, and the whole regiment must share in the prize money, so I suppose you can afford a million, eh?'

"'Oh dear no, your Excellency!' cried the poor old fellow, falling on his knees. 'I haven't a tenth part of that. Oh, spare me and my girls, take your jewellery and all you can 6nd in the house!'

" 'Pooh! pooh, man! I'm inclined to be reasonable, but it can't be less than half a million at least, if you don't agree to that your daughters shall frig you till you confess where the money is to come from,' replied the colonel, with a grin of sardonic pleasure, especially when he noticed the blushing horror of the young ladies at his outrageous words.

"Lord Dufferstones was ordered to stand up, and told that it was useless for him to persist in his lies, about inability to pay, to which our chief added his opinion, 'that probably the daughters of such an old liar were only mock modest after all.'

"The old man trembled like an aspen in abject fear of what might be going to happen, whilst the girls hid their crimson faces from sight, and sobbed with indignant shame.

"The old sergeant now re-appeared with a couple of good birch rods, canes, whips, and scourges, all of which he informed us had been found in the housekeeper's room, below, in a cupboard, and added to the colonel, I find, sir, he is a lord, and has been in the habit of inHicting personal chastisement on the bare bottoms of the young servant girls, or boy pages, with the assistance of his housekeeper, who always had complaints to make and faults to find which needed correction. They always carried it out on afternoons when the young ladies were gone out for a drive, so this is their stock in trade, laying his bundle on a table close at hand.

"'Very fine, indeed,' laughed the old German, as he turned again towards the prisoners, 'you sergeant, give the housekeeper a good taste of the whip, amuse yourselves by making the youngest servants insult and Hog her; up here we will let these English aristocrats know what it is to suffer such degrading punishments, and so you are a Milord, a proud noble, but I can see you're a coward; out with your dirty old cock, sir, and show it to your pretty mincing mock modest daughters, let them see their real papa. Ha! ah! ! what a joke!'

"His lordship moaned, his horror and surprise were really too great for words.

"'Come here, young lady, take your hands from your face, and tell me your name, no nonsense or I will have your skin cut off your bot-torn by your own father's whips and rods,' said the chief sternly to the eldest girl.

"'Nora, my name is Nora Dufferstones, your Excellency, oh, have mercy on us and our poor old father!" exclaimed that young lady, starting forward, and throwing herself at his feet, with all the abandon of despair.

" 'Nora, eh! a very pretty Irish name; ahem, get up my dear, you see the helpless state of your papa, with his hands tied behind his back; it's a very delicate thing to mention, but I'm an old soldier, you won't mind me, my dear, the fact is these gentlemen, — hem, yes, these German officers want you and your sisters to see your papa's cock, the real author of your being, you observe he is unable to get it out himself, so please unfasten his front, and pull it out. Ha! you hesitate to obey, I did not want to be severe, get up and do as I tell you, this — this very instant, you English bitch,' as he spurned her from him, and spat in her face.

"The poor girl was awfully abashed at this violence and insult, sobbing, crying, blushing, and indignant all at the same time, whilst her two younger sisters, Ringing their arms around her neck, added their cries and sobs to hers.

"You would have thought such a scene as this would melt the sternest hearts to pity, but on the contrary it excited every one present, and I do not believe but that every one wished to prolong their sense of smarting humiliation; at least I can say my prick was bursting in my trousers, in fact all the young officers seemed wrought up to an equal state of voluptuous emotion; even their own father, bound and a prisoner as he was, seemed to derive pleasure at the sight of their agonized distress.

"'No more of this, girls!' shouted the old German in a furious voice, 'will one of you do as I tell you immediately. By Jove! you shall suck your father's prick till he spends, for not minding my orders!' he had taken up a small sharp cutting whip, and was slashing the three sisters without mercy, over their heads, necks, or faces, several of the cuts drawing blood; the poor victims shrieking in helpless terror, clinging yet closer together, as the blood streamed from the broken weals on their tender and delicate flesh.

"'Now look up at these, gentlemen,' he resumed, dropping the whip from his hand, 'I believe they are about to shower their love juice upon you.'

"Every prick in the room (except his lordship's) was out, and there were fourteen or fifteen red-headed bursting penises presented to the gaze of the horrified girls as we closely surrounded our prisoners, frigging ourselves, and shoving them close to their mouths, noses, or eyes, so that our spendings deluged the blood-stained faces, or went down their gasping throats.

" 'Horrible! Nasty! Disgusting!' they shrieked in chorus.

" 'Then do as I order you at once!" thundered the colonel. 'Lady Nora, unbutton your father's breeches; Lady Kathleen, you put in your hand and pull out his cock, and you my little innocent Lady Ellen shall pull back his wicked old foreskin and frig him. Now be quick, what is the use of pretending to be so shocked and mock modest? Ha! ha! ! As if I don't know how the young ladies play with each other's cunnies, or examine the cocks of the pages in these aristocratic mansions, why I am given to understand they are very hot beds of sensuality!'

" 'He had again taken up the terrible whip, and was pointing them to the task with it, but seeing their determined reluctance to obey, he threw it aside, and ordering us to tie the old man down in a chair, then asked us to stretch the three young ladies on the floor face downwards, and to slap their obstinate arses till they were obedient.

"The colonel sat down, and there were at least three of us to each of the victims, so we arranged them with their bottoms towards him, Lady Nora in the centre, and a sister on each side of her. How they kicked and screamed as we deliberately and slowly turned up their skirts, first discovering their beautiful legs encased in white silk stockings, through which the tint of their flesh could almost be seen, whilst

their small feet and elegant chaussures quite enchanted us. We pulled their drawers open behind to show the marble whiteness of their

buttocks, and rucked them up so as also to expose nearly half of their beautifully developed thighs.

"They were all three very lovely brunettes, with very dark brown hair, and hazel eyes shaded by long dark lashes, which added to

their Gushed faces, and tearful, frightened looks, made a sight to stir the blood of the most icy temperament you could imagine.

" 'Now,' said the colonel, 'I want to make sure of not missing the sight if the slapping makes them spend, so please tie an ankle of each of the younger sisters to the ankle of Lady Nora, and then two of you at the outside can keep all their legs well open. It's delicious to watch the quivering of their pretty little cunts at every slap, as the excitement and heat of their parts increases.'

"How pretty the three bottoms looked, with just a glimpse of tight little wrinkled brown bum-holes, and the slits underneath; the two eldest fairly ornamented with dark silky hair, whilst the youngest, Lady Ellen, had only a suspicion of down upon her sweetly interesting paraphernalia of love. I was holding the untied leg of the latter, so was close enough to study all the minutiae of what her position exposed to view.

"'Are you all ready?' asked the old German, 'then three of you kneel across their backs, with your faces to their rumps, and be ready to slap as I count, and be sure to keep good time, or I will select others the next time we have a treat of this kind to enjoy. Now—one—two—three

"So beautifully was it done that the smacks fell like a cracking volley, the victims screaming and kicking in pain and humiliation at every slap.

" 'Delightful! -— deli — ci — ous! — de — li — ci — ous!' exclaimed the colonel, his face glowing with pleasurable emotions. 'Look at their crimson faces, streaming eyes, and heaving bums; watch the kicking and twisting of their lovely limbs. See now, look closer as I go on. Four — five — six — seven — eight. Ha, that's prime, splendid indeed! Lady Nora's already spending; did you notice how the lips of their cunts opened and twitched at every impact of the hand. Now let them get up, and see if they will obey my orders, but mind tie up all their skirts well above their waists, and put the tails of their chemises well away, so as that we may enjoy the sight of their bums and cunts where the drawers are open.'

"It was a delightfully ludicrous sight when the three girls stood blushing in front of our old colonel, with their skirts tied in a knot behind, just above their waists, cunnies and bums peeping out from the opening of their drawers in front or behind, as we happened to view them.

" 'Well, girls,' the colonel went on, 'now you have had a taste of what we can do with obstinate husseys like yourselves, are you inclined to carry out my orders, or must we proceed to more cruel extremities?'

"They all sank on their knees again, and with streaming eyes, begged in the most piteous manner that his excellency would have mercy on them and their poor old father, praying expeciâlly to be spared the degrading shocking test of obedience suggested in the order.

" 'Then why is he such an obstinate old fool? Don't talk to me about inability to pay the halfmillion ransom, I know every one in this square has hundreds of thousands a year; the long and the short of it is you shall frig him to death if he does not promise the money, do you think the Germans have come here not to enrich themselves?'

"Seeing their utter state of confusion and bewilderment, he rose from his seat and took up the little whip again. 'Now girls, you English bitches shall find that old Cuntswigger, Colonel Cuntswigger I should say, of the Pomeranian Guards, is a man of his word? I do mean you to do it, so now begin — begin — begin!' slashing each of them in turn, till the blood dripped down the inside of their drawers, plainly showing by the stained marks, the terrible force of his cuts. 'It's no use shrieking for mercy!' as he laughed at their frantic cries, 'the only way to get off is to begin the task, your minds are altogether wrong, or it would delight and give you pleasure to play with a prick, especially your father's!'

"Old Dufferstones was so excited that he fairly groaned at the sight of his daughters' distress and humiliated agony, whilst his big prick, old and debilitated as he almost always seemed, was swollen and throbbing in his breeches.

"Catching sight of him, the colonel called on us all to help, so without mercy the three sisters were pushed and dragged up to the old man's chair, where he sat with his hands tied behind him, quite helpless, but as red as a turkey cock and glaring with excitement.

"We first pointed out to them the fine erection which was so plainly visible, the colonel giving the old man's prick a very painful cut as he drew their attention to it; then one of the officers took Lady Nora's hand and made her stroke and feel how her father's affair throbbed under her touch. She closed her eyes but re-opened them with a start of horror, as some one behind suddenly rammed his finger into her bottom-hole, and

34

turning round tried to box the ears of her fundamental ravisher, exclaiming with great indignation, 'Monster, how shameful, would you outrage me so?'

" 'Bravo, you're a spirited girl, but a fool!' laughed the old German, 'that young gentleman only wants to give you pleasure, my dear; go on boys, give them a good bottom frigging!'

"It is impossible to describe the delightful scene which followed, an officer on each side held the girls' hands, which they would place on the old man's prick, or make them feel their own, whilst a third one behind was busy with his finger in their bums; our cocks were let out and placed in their hands, and we made them see how we spent, then insisted they should suck their slimy fingers clean, and taste the fingers of the gentlemen who had had them up their bottoms; they were awfully shocked and distressed, yet we could plainly see that all three of them were sensually excited by what they had seen and felt behind.

" 'Now, this is all play, and papa is waiting for his turn; after all, my dears, you are not nearly so loving as the daughters of old Lot, who made their father tight and then seduced him to fuck them. Mein Gott, it must have been delicious for the old fellow!'

"Nora was brought as close as possible to her father, and ordered to unbutton his trousers, the colonel cutting her hands with the whip, and not at all mindful if he hit her papa's affair as he did so; at last she seemed to comply in a At of desperation, and actually swooned away as his big cock burst into view slimy with spend, and stained with blood from some of the colonel's reckless cuts, which had slightly abraded the tender skin of the prepuce.

" 'We'll soon bring your sister round, Lady Kathleen, but you must first kiss and stroke your real papa,' continued old Cuntswigger, as we made her take old Dufferstone's cock in her hand, and pressed her head down till she kissed it. Then she was allowed to stand aside whilst we forced the young Lady Ellen to take papa's Priapus in her mouth, as the colonel with a fine birch switched her backside to make her do it properly.

"Whilst this was going on, I got so excited that seeing Lady Nora lying on the carpet quite unconscious, I threw myself upon her, and forcing her legs apart, drove my Aery steed at the outworks of her virginity; the sudden shock at once brought her round, so as to realise the situation in a moment. With a scream of horror she struggled so violently as almost to throw me out, but I had the head fairly lodged, and enfolded her in my arms as tight as a boa constrictor. Another furious lunge and I felt she was conquered, and at the same time spurted a tremendous gush of spend into her womb, just as she swooned again. It was delightful to me, the painful and hard won victory seemed to make my enjoyment tenfold more delicious, as my cock soaked and throbbed within the soft, yet tightly contracted folds of her vagina.

" 'Pull him off!' shouted old Cuntswigger, 'how dare you sir, without orders, thank your stars you do not belong to the 2nd Pomeranians!'

"Instantly they dragged me from the darling Nora, who I had so long secretly loved, to be revelling in her cunt seemed the very scene of bliss. My prick was still distended in the most lustful manner, and stained with a mixture of my spendings and her virgin blood, but what was my surprise when in an instant old Cuntswigger was down on his knees gamahuching me in the most delightful manner, sucking, smacking his lips, and enjoying the taste of my prick with the greatest gusto, till I almost choked him with another delicious emission. He swallowed every drop, and then letting me go, said, as he licked his foaming lips, "Ha, my boy, I wouldn't have missed that treat for my share of the prize money; it's really the only thing I can now enjoy, the blood and spendings from a reeking prick which has just taken a maidenhead. Now get into her again, and let us enjoy the sight of seeing you work her up to the highest pitch of sensual excitement.'

"She was just opening her eyes and coming to herself, when I rammed my prick into her again with tremendous force, which at once made her painfully realise how she was placed; her pale features were instantly suffused with the deepest crimson, as she ground her teeth in an agony of rage, shame, and as I guessed, impotent desires for revenge, even biting her lovely lips till the blood came.

"Ah, Nora, dear Lady Nora!" I almost screamed with delight, as my arms pressed her body to mine with all the strength I could so well exert in my erotic fury, "I know it is cruel, but the very pain you suffer confers on me the greatest pleasure, your crimson cheeks and blood-stained lips only add to my voluptuous ardour, whilst my happy prick revels in the blood of your ravished virginity, I will also suck some of it from your inviting lips!" as I glued my lips to hers, almost sucking her breath away. "Don't you begin to feel a little forgiveness now, dear Nora? Are your feelings dead to the stirring emotions of love? See, I am not afraid to trust the tip of my tongue between your teeth." My motions now began to have a slight effect, and this tipping the velvet seemed to add marvellously to the incipient excitement, the hitherto slight motions of her buttocks in response to the thrusts of King Priapus, suddenly quickened into almost frantic bounds, threatening to unseat her active rider, who fortunately was able to hold on, and go the pace the impetuous steed plunged into.

"Old Cuntswigger was in extasies, he knelt down behind us, forced one finger up my arsehole, part of the same hand tickling my balls; his other hand was equally busy with Nora, postillioning her bottom in the most exciting way, with one digit, whilst the next one was inside her deliciously tight cunt, feeling how my prick was going on, and adding greatly to our enjoyment.

"This was too good to last long, we came together in tremendous gushes of sperm, which churned into whitish troth as our motions continued, oozing out on his fingers, which he took pleasure in licking one after the other, urging us not to stop but to go on again without resting to recover ourselves, but seeing I was rather Ragging after such an extraordinary bout, he

37

ordered some one to freshen me up with a birch rod. That ended my dream, for the first cut was such a stinging whacker that I awoke with a start."

CHAPTER III

Conclusion of the Evening,
Spencer reads his Tale of of Vanessa.

"And quite as well," exclaimed Fuckatilla, "it was beginning to get painfully cruel. I like tender love best."

"So do I, that is exactly what I think, although a few skilful strokes of the twigs are delicious provocatives to sensual enjoyment, I don't like going to extremes," said Spencer. "Now I vote for a bit of fun, then I will read you a tale called Vanessa, which I have got ready especially for this evening, and trust you may approve of its not too florid style, as I have tried to write it something in the style of 'Fanny Hill'."

"I shall call on Jack Turdey for a song first. Mind, my boy, it is one of the newest out," said their host.

"You shall have, 'Under the Garden Wall,' I got it at a convivial a night or two ago," said Jack, clearing his throat, "here goes!"

UNDER THE GARDEN WALL

I went to piss 'gainst a walnut tree,
Under the Garden Wall,
When I saw such a sight that startled me,

Under the Garden Wall, At first it was dark,
but I soon made out,
Under the Garden Wall,
A male and a female were there without doubt;
Under the Garden Wall,
I wasn't long guessing what they were about,
Under the Garden Wall. CHORUS: —
Under the garden wall, the fellow was young
and tall; The lady was fair beyond compare, she little
suspected that I was there; Her clothes were up,
and her arse was bare! Under the Garden Wall.
I saw she'd a pair of delightful thighs,
Under the Garden Wall;
And he had a prick of enormous size,
Under the Garden Wall;
I heard her exclaim, "What a beauty, dear Jim!
Be quick you old ducky, and do put him in;
Go gently at first, or you'll split my young quim,
Under the Garden Wall. CHORUS: —
Under, &c. I then heard a groan, and I then heard a grunt,
Under the Garden Wall;
Said she, "How I love you to tickle my cunt,
Under the Garden Wall;
The sight gave me palpitation of the heart,
When I saw how she squirmed on his blooming dart,
With excitement, when one of them let a loud fart,
Under the Garden Wall. CHORUS: —
Under, &c. My prick got stiff 'gainst the walnut tree,
Under the Garden Wall; And I found no inclination to pee,
Under the Garden Wall; The sight gave me a peculiar shock,
I found myself rubbing my sensitive jock,
They had real turtle, and I had the mock,
Under the Garden Wall. CHORUS: — Under, &c.

"That's something like a song, can't you, Mr. Bigcock, sing us another?" said the vivacious Nelly, who had joined heartily in the chorus.

"No, you little darling!" laughed their host, "but I will just give you a new Aesthetic Nursery Rhyme, and then have Mr. Spencer's tale."

An Aesthetic young miss of Calcutta, Set all the men's hearts in a flutter,

Her bubs were intense,

Her arse was immense, And her cunt quite too utterly utter!

Taking up his manuscript, "My tale," said the reader, "is called 'Vanessa, the Story of a Milliner's Apprentice, or Memoirs of a Lady of Pleasure in London'."

INTRODUCTION

To the Reader,—

The subject of these pages is a very fashionable beauty in Kensington at the present time; long since, when I first made her acquaintance she promised to write out all the most interesting incidents in her life, and at last I have prevailed upon her to keep her word, and am thus enabled to make public a most interesting story of a real lady of pleasure, from the days of her youth and poverty up to the present time, when she is now one of the shining lights of the highest circle of the Demi-Monde.

THE AUTHOR

VANESSA, &C.

CHAPTER I

Apprenticeship, &c.

I WAS BORN IN A WORKHOUSE, IN THE WEST of English, my poor mother giving up her last breath as she gave me life. An orphan from my

birth, who never even knew who her father was.

Like the celebrated Cora Pearl, who lately married a rich nobleman in Paris, after having been the bright particular star amongst *les files du monde* of that great city; I also had a very common name, hers, I believe, was Emma Crutch, mine nothing more than Phoebe Smith, the same as my poor mother's.

Well, to go on with my story. I believe that as I got out of babyhood I grew so intelligent and pretty that I became a general pet amongst all the officials of the workhouse master, matron, doctor, etc., everyone seemed to take an interest in little Phoebe, and thanks to natural quickness, my education was far better than usually the result of such surroundings, but you may guess I had many very curious adventures even in my earliest days of girlhood.

The matron often sent me messages to the rector and others in our village, as she knew it gave me pleasure to run out now and then.

Our rector was a nice old gentleman, nearly eighty years of age, and he would often ask me into his study, under pretence of examining me, to see how my education was going on. The old man really seemed to feel his feet a little during these visits, and generally gave me sixpence for a nice kiss before he would let me go. Of course I was always glad to go to the rectory, especially as Mrs. Wilson, the housekeeper, often gave me sweets and cakes in addition to the parson's sixpences.

At last I was upon quite familiar terms with him, and used frequently to sit on his knee and kiss him, as he called me a dear little pet, and very frequently his hands would go up under my clothes, till they felt my thighs and even something else, as he explained to me what a pity and shame it was that the guardians did not allow drawers, "You would look so pretty little Phoebe, properly dressed," he would say and go on all the while taking liberties which at the time my innocence did not see any harm in.

I was nearly ten years old, when one day, our matron told me that Mrs. Wilson at the rectory wanted me to help her for the afternoon, if I could be spared, "so you had better make yourself nice, and go at once, my dear," and I did not want telling twice.

The old parson was delighted to see me.

"Mrs. Wilson sent for my pet to spend the afternoon with me, as she is going out, and I have such a surprise for you, Phoebe," he said.

The housekeeper was soon gone, and I now believe it was a

regular planned thing between them, as when he died he left her a house and two pounds a week for life.

Leaving my straw hat and cloak in Mrs. Wilson's room, he led me to the study, where he took me on his knee and almost stifled me with kisses.

"What do you think I have got for my pet?" he asked.

"Is that all you think of, Phoebe? Wouldn't you like to see yourself in fine clothes, eh?"

I jumped off his knee in delight, as I clapped my hands, exclaiming, "You old dear, let me see them, I don't believe you have got them!"

"Open that parcel there, and I must help you put them on," he said, pointing to a large brown paper package on a chair in one corner, the end of it was there was a complete outfit, little low necked silk dresses, stays, petticoats, drawers, chemise, etc., trimmed with lace, and even silk stockings, and such beautiful little slippers with high heels and buckles of silver.

How his hands trembled as he helped me first to strip, and then to put on all this finery which quite fired my young imagination, and made me think of the possibility of yet being a real lady, as I knew I was beautiful. Even when quite naked it banished all ideas of anything wrong, I only thought the old parson was fond of his pet, and wanted to please me.

His hands wandered over every part of me, before the dressing was commenced, then when I stood before him, only dressed as far as my stays, petticoats, and drawers, he took no end of time turning me round and examining if everything fitted properly.

Then he began to tell me what a naughty boy he was, that I ought to play at being schoolmistress, and whip him well.

The fun of the thing took possession of me at once, and as he had often shown me a birch rod, and said he would use it some day if ever he found me a naughty girl, I knew the drawer where I could lay my hand upon it.

"So I will, you bad boy, I know where Tickle Toby is kept," I said, getting the rod out.

He took it from my hand, and said, "Now, Miss Phoebe, don't spare my bottom. I have been so naughty, and if you do it nicely you shall soon come to live with us, and be my schoolmistress very often."

Nothing would do but I must take his breeches down and birch him well, which at last I did, and he was so impudent, and tried all he could to irritate me by calling me "a cruel little wretch, an ugly thing, etc.," that I paid him out finely. The scene always amuses and tickles my fancy even after all these years, and I do not know to what lengths we might have gone after a while, had not the poor old rector died very soon after, and so dispelled all my dreams of finery, etc., for a time.

One of my best qualities has always been secrecy as to what I did, so no one, unless it was Mrs. Wilson, even guessed at my game with the rector, poor old fellow.

The master of the workhouse was in the habit of inflicting personal chastisement on any of the boy or girl inmates who gave cause for correction, this I had long known and now felt quite a curiosity to see how he managed it, especially with the big girls and boys.

This could only be accomplished by hiding myself in a small ante-chamber which led into Mr. Watson's business room; there was a halfglass door with a curtain, which I could easily draw on one side and peep. The further side of the master's room had a staircase leading to a work-room, so that each culprit entered at one door and was sent away to work by the other.

Mondays the girls were whipped, and Wednesdays he birched the troublesome lads or boys. I suppose it was only natural that I should most wish to see a boy stripped, so the first Wednesday I could manage it I shut myself in an empty cupboard in the ante-room about the usual whipping time, and soon heard Mr. W------and the

matron, Mrs. Jones, bring a boy for punishment. The door was locked on the inside, and I crept from the closet, and pulling one corner of the blind aside, could see everything, and quite safe from being seen myself, unless they especially looked towards the door, even then I felt sure I could escape without being caught

With what stillness I kept at my post! fearing that the least noise might attract the attention of either of them, but I had not much reason to fear, for they were both of them so much taken up with the business in hand, that they had no notion of thinking about *espionage*. Yet I trembled from head to foot, with an indescribable apprehension, not so much of fear as that I might see something almost too bad to look at, as I knew the master was such a strict man in carrying out his punishments. I could see everything, and a corner being broken out of one of the glass panes in the door, I could hear equally well. The culprit was a fine lad of about sixteen, and they set about tying his hands above his head to a clothes hook, high up the wall one side of the room, so I had an excellent view of him *en profile*.

"I guess you'll remember this for some time, or my name's not Watson!" said the master, almost grinding his teeth, he appeared in such a rage.

"Pray be cool, sir," said the matron, "don't let your temper carry you away, no doubt the boy's been very insulting to both of us, and well deserves what you will give him, only think of his calling you an old b----r, and me a bitch — indeed, when I'm so kind to every one in the house!"

Although she talked to him about being cool, she looked very Rushed herself, as she helped to pull down the lad's breeches, thus exposing to my view all the male paraphernalia of manhood, slightly adorned with a fringe of soft dark hair, evidently only recently just beginning to grow.

"Now he's ready for the birch," she said, with a chuckle, as she finished pinning up the tail of his shirt, and pulled the breeches quite down to the culprit's knees.

"Yes, I think it's my turn now, Simpson," said Mr. Watson, who had taken a heavy bunch of birch from a cupboard, "you will soon be sorry for your laziness and impudence, I feel quite kindly towards him now, Mrs. Jones, it's really wonderful how my feelings are soothed as soon as I take the swishtail in hand."

His face was quite changed from the angry look it had a minute or two before, as he took up his position behind the culprit, who had been strictly mute so far.

No more time was lost, Mr. Watson's soul was very evidently in his work — swish -— crash —swish — crash —-swish — crash —that is what the blows sounded like to me, as he gave a sweeping flourish through the air at each stroke. The third blow elicited a subdued wincing cry from the lad.

"That's it, why don't you give it mouth, Simpson, as you did when you abused me and Mrs. Jones?" he exclaimed. "Does it cut you a little, my boy? Will you abuse us again, eh?'

This last was followed by a tremendous crasher, which drew little drops of blood from the wealed flesh, then blow followed blow, soon making the drops into little rills which fairly trickled over his buttocks and down his thighs, whilst poor Simpson's cries were awful to hear, mixed as they were with the swishing and crashing of the rod. How the poor fellow did beg for mercy, but all to no avail, the master was relentless, and cut away as if it was nothing much, jeering and lecturing the boy all the while.

Now my eyes fairly started, for there was young Simpson's affair sticking out rampant and redheaded in front of him, in fact I seemed to fancy that the boy purposely rubbed himself against the wall as every cut of the birch drove him forward, his cries ceased, and I could not make it out, but just then Mrs. Jones coming behind the master, put her arms round to his front, and unbuttoning Mr. Watson's breeches, exposed to my full view an enormous affair, nine or ten inches long, which she played with in her hands, passing them rapidly up and down the long white shaft, uncovering at every motion the ruby head of what looked quite a monster to me then, all the while agitating and rubbing her belly against his back as she did so. It only lasted for about a couple of minutes, then I saw quite a jet of thick whitish stuff spurt from him right on to the boy's raw bottom, who evidently was unconscious of what was going on behind him,

After this she buttoned him up again, and then Simpson was let down and cautioned as to his future conduct, and what he would get next time, then ordered to be 08 to his work, and sent away through the further door, which I have mentioned.

Of course I thought it was all over, and should have slipped away from my point of observation, had not Mr. Watson seized Mrs. Jones round the waist and borne her to a couch, kissing her, and putting his hands under her clothes till I got a glimpse of a splendid naked thigh.

"Was it nice, Dick? Did I give you pleasure, dear?" I heard her murmur.

"Heavenly, delightful, my love! And now it's my turn to repay you, open your lovely thighs and let me see what you know I love to kiss so!" he replied, pulling her willing legs apart, and regularly burying his face in what I then thought was a very dirty place.

She closed her eyes, and lay back almost as if in a faint, but one hand was pressing his head to keep him as it were to his work, whilst the other with clenched fist hung down by her side.

"Ah — r — r — re, Oh, oh. Lovely — delightful. Go on you darling. There -— there —just on the little spot. Ah —-r — r — re, I'm going to come. Oh —oh," I could hear her say in gasping accents, and then saw her stiffen herself out in a listless state.

He kissed or sucked on eagerly for a moment or two, then jumping up, knelt on the bench between her legs, his great thing sticking out in front of his belly from a profusion of dark hair, which adorned that part of his person. He opened Mrs. Jones' thighs till I could quite see her love gap with pouting vermillion lips glistening with moisture, then to my astonishment he directed the head of his big engine, and opening those lips with one hand actually shoved the whole length of the tremendous thing up into her belly, till it was buried out of sight.

This seemed to wake up the matron, for suddenly throwing her arms round Mr. Watson, she heaved up her bottom to meet his thrusts, which he for his part was quite ready to respond to, kissing her face and lips ardently all the while, till after a few minutes both of them seemed as it were, to melt away, and lay listless in each other's arms.

Now was my time to slip away, which I did, but what an impression that scene had upon me, it thrilled my whole soul, and circulated a fire through every vein of my body, which increased so violently as almost to prevent respiration.

I was now only too well disposed, young as I still was to enter into any rude game that might offer with my own or the opposite sex.

I had a little bed-fellow, Sarah Marsh, about my own age, her I admitted to my confidence, and we resolved the very first chance to have a game ourselves with one of the boys.

It so happened that in a day of two was the annual treat, and we all went to the park attached to the hall to spend the day.

The village squire was a liberal man, the grown-up paupers, both old and young, were regaled to their hearts content, whilst the children ran about at pleasure in the grounds or a large wooded dell in the dark. Sarah and myself selected a pretty boy of about twelve for our sweetheart, and told Johnny Stones (that was his name), that we had something so nice to let him into.

Soon finding ourselves in a place quite free from observation, we told him the story about Mr. Watson and Mrs. Jones, and asked him to try and do the same for us; he was seated on the grass eating a cake so we soon had his little pintle out, it stood almost directly, and he tried to get into first one and then the other of us, but it hurt so much we had to give it up, and contented ourselves by sucking and kissing each other's affairs, which we thought very nice. ' Suddenly, "Haw, haw — ha, ha — here's a go," startled us from our game.

"Don't be frightened dears," said a kind voice. 'I'll give you a shilling each to let me play with you."

It was Squire Benson himself, and the sight of the bright silver soon made us at our ease, and we promised never to tell a word.

He made us unbutton and get out his affair, but what a contrast to the workhouse master's grand instrument, Mr. Benson's was a little thing only a trifle 6ve inches in length, but he was delighted to have us handle and kiss it, then laughing when we told him all about Mr. Watson and the matron, and how we had failed in our endeavours to get Johnny's thing into us, he told us he could tell a much better way which would do no harm, as the front way made babies; then he made me kneel all fours on the grass, and took Johnny's pintle into his mouth, wetting it first with his saliva before he made him shove at my bottom-hole, it soon slipped in, and my boy kneeling behind me with his arms round my belly, worked away in the vent-hole, and gave me exquisite pleasure; meanwhile the Squire telling my partner not to mind a slight pinch, soon planted his own affair in Johnny's bum, whilst he made Sarah tickle and play with him, and put her finger up his own bottom.

We kept at this game for a long time, till it was beginning to get almost dusk, I did not feel anything myself, except an exquisite titillation of the anus, but Johnny told me he felt the Squire quite plainly as he twice emitted into him, and that it was lovely and warm.

Our sweetheart was sent to a situation soon after this, and Sarah and myself remaining constant friends we kept our secret to ourselves, and varied our amusement as much as possible, using Angers or tongues as the fancy took us, still we were very careful, for fear of being found out, and did not run into any very great excesses.

Soon after I was twelve years old they put me out to be nursemaid in the family of Farmer Royston. He was the grandest man of the village after the squire and the rector, having a large farm and a 6ne water mill as well.

Mr. Royston was a widower, who had recently lost his wife, who left him with a rather large family of all ages, from sixteen to two years old, the household being now presided over by a Miss Mabel Wilberforce, in the double capacity of housekeeper and governess.

Master Charlie, the eldest, went to school, and only came home for the holidays, as also did the Misses Gertrude and Lily, who were fourteen and thirteen respectively, besides these there were Ave younger ones with whom I had more specially to do under the supervision of Miss Wilberforce; the farmer was a jolly fine man, not yet forty I should say, and had such a way of talking to or looking at the girls, that anyone could not be slow to see, that he had a considerable amount of human nature about him.

I ' slept in the nursery with the children, Mr. Royston and the housekeeper occupying two rooms on the same floor, whilst three maidservants slept in an attic above, where there was also a couple of small rooms, only used during the holidays for the accommodation of Master Charlie and his two elder sisters.

Amongst my other duties I had to wait at table, and it did not take me long to 6nd out that a very tender tie of some sort existed between the farmer and his housekeeper, for he always called her "my dear," and treated her with every possible mark of deference, and in fact she ruled him, as well as everything else in the house.

Before I had been a week in the house I came upon them accidently one day in the garden, they were quite unaware of being observed, he was kissing her tenderly, and I heard him say, "Then, dear Mabel, you promise to make me happy to-night?" her face was averted and looking down, but I could hear a soft "yes" in reply.

Not doubting but a real love scene would be enacted between them that night, I slipt away, resolving in my mind how it might be possible to be a spectatress of their transports, as I had of the amours of Mr. Watson and the matron of the workhouse.

Running up to the nursery I examined every part to see if there was any prospect of getting a sight into Miss Mabel's room, which was next to it, in one corner there was a clothes closet, which gave me a presentiment of some sort of access to the next apartment, and imagine my pleasure when I found that the back of it was evidently a door of communication with the key to the other side, so I ran round into her room and discovered a similar closet, not locked, so that I could enter and unlock the door, which I found opened easily and noiselessly for my purpose. As there was no handle on my side I took the key, so as to be able to open it when I pleased.

Her bed was in a small alcove, opposite to this closet, and the outer door of the closet I found had a small round hole, where a knot had fallen out of the wood, forming a splendid peephole for observation on everything that might be done by her or her lover.

Night came, and I was on the tip-toe of expectation. Retiring to rest with the children, I kept awake till I heard Miss Wilberforce enter her room, then getting out of bed put on my stockings and crept to the place of observation.

She had loosened her hair, which fell in long wavy golden masses all over her shoulders, as she sat in a low chair looking at a small book. She had a lovely pale Grecian type of face, which Hushed with evident blushes every now and then, as she turned over the pages.

Presently I saw it drop from her hands, as she nervously raised her clothes, and seemed to me to be titillating her most private charms, as I heard her say with a sigh, "What a time he is coming. Why did he give me such a book?"

Just then I observed Mr. Royston quietly enter the room behind her, so that he was almost touching her back before she was aware of it. He had nothing but his shirt on.

"Mabel, love, I'm in such a state, and you, darling, are not even undressed yet!" he said in a low voice.

She turned with a start.

"Oh, Mr. Royston, how you startle me. Oh, for shame, sir, to expose yourself so!" as he raised his shirt, and let her see his Cupid's battering ram in a glorious state of erection. It was a tremendous affair, quite ten inches long, as thick as my wrist, and tipped with a fierylooking purple head, which I can only describe as being mushroom shaped, in fact I have never seen such an engine of love ever since, it was perfectly unique in its style as far as my varied experience goes.

"What a monster, and can such an awful looking thing as that give me pleasure, and can I make you happy by submitting to its ravages in my tenderest parts? Mr. Royston, you know I told you that I had been seduced by my cousin two years ago, who failed in his promise to marry me, after I was so foolish as to surrender my virtue. His was only an ordinary sized shaft of love, and gave me intense pleasure, the recollections of which only made me too easily listen to your tender proposals, and, besides, I admit that your book has had a most demoralising effect on me, in fact I was quite ardently longing for you to come and ease the warmth of a certain little spot, but it's all gone now, the sight of such a tremendous thing quite frightens away all thoughts of love!"

"Nonsense, Mabel darling," he replied, falling on his knees in front of her, and taking her hand in his, printing hot impassioned kisses for a moment or two, then went on, "Why so afraid, you know the joys of love, my size will only enable me to give you greater pleasure, the fuller your little purse is gorged by my big shaft the greater extasy for my love, no girl was ever mortally or even seriously wounded in that dear spot, which even now I know must be palpitating and fluttering with unsatisfied expectations of bliss. Besides, my love, you shall find me so gentle and careful not to hurt you in any way, we will use a little cold cream to facilitate affairs, and after one insertion all will be joy and love unspeakable. Come, darling, let me assist to undress my pet!"

She was helpless in his hands, I could see she feared her fate, and yet was drawn towards it by some irristable fascination.

Presently he had her as naked as the day she was born. Then throwing off his own shirt, he took her in his brawny arms and carried her to the bed.

What a contrast between them; his almost Herculean frame, the muscles of his legs and arms, and back standing out in fine relief, a veritable study for a sculptor. He was a dark handsome man, close shaved, with fine black bushy whiskers, his bosom ornamented in the centre and round the paps with quite a profusion of hair so strongly indicative of manly vigour, whilst his mushroom-headed stag projected from a perfect profusion of black curls at the bottom of his belly. His inamorata, a pretty blonde with golden hair, blue eyes, with a rather light graceful figure, just plump enough to make a pretty *tournure*, small round firm bosoms, with delicious little strawberry nipples, which looked so impudently inviting as almost to distract the attention from the charms of her Mons Veneris, covered as it was with soft downy light hair, which hardly shaded an almost imperceptible crack, just visible at the bottom of her belly.

She still had on her slippers, silk stockings, and pretty garters, which added greatly to her generally ravishing appearance. I hate naked feet, they are so much prettier when properly dressed, and I fancy the majority of my readers are of the same opinion.

Instead of placing her on the middle of the bed, he let her down on the edge, so that if she had sat up her feet would just have touched the floor, then inclining her body backwards he gently opened that pretty pair of legs till I could plainly see the cherry lips of a lovely tight looking love grot, which he speedily began to kiss, as if he would eat it.

How she squirmed and twisted under that lascivious tongueing, till I could hear her sigh out? "You darling, what heavenly pleasure you give me. Oh — oh — oh!! I can't help it, you make me come, you dear man. Now try your affair, love, and be gentle, I do want you so, you've made me feel so, so naughty, you dear fellow!"

He was up from his knees in a moment, and taking some pomatum from a pot on the toilet table, lubricated that mushroom-headed affair, till it glistened in the candle-light, then quickly presenting it to the dear spot he had been so amorously kissing a moment or two before, and opening those luscious looking lips as well as he could with his fingers, I was tremendously astonished to see him soon get it all into her, although certainly to judge by the expression of her face it was not quite a painless operation.

She threw her legs over his buttocks and clasped him

amorously with her arms, as he laid over her body and joined his lips to hers in long sucking kisses, making (as I now imagine) that tremendous affair of his throb inside of her tight-fitting sheath, till she was almost beside herself with lust, and heaved up her bottom as a challenge to him to start on his ride.

His first thrust made her scream with pain, and beg him to be more gentle, but after going at quarter speed for a few strokes, he gradually put on the steam, till both seemed perfectly furious, as he thrust and she heaved up to meet every plunge of that awful weapon, just as if it was nothing out of the common. I could hear the concussion at every stroke as his piston rod was sheathed to the hilt, and the bag of treasures below banged against her beautiful rump. Their kisses and sighs, or exclamations of delight mingled with the other sounds, and the creaking of the bed, all put together so moved the blood in my veins that lifting my night-dress, my hands were soon busy rubbing the electrical spot till we all seemed to melt away in an extasy of bliss at the same moment.

It was too much for me, I fairly fainted, and falling down in the closet, aroused them from their delicious after lethargy. Mr. Royston must have run away, but Miss Wilberforce dragged me from the closet, and when I came to a little I found myself lying on her bed, she had assumed her *chemise de nuit*, and was holding a smelling bottle to my nose.

You may be sure I was awfully frightened, but she soon reassured me by promise of forgiveness, so that I told her all.

I shall never forget that woman, her blood was on fire; she told me I had spoilt her amusement for the rest of the night, and must make up for it by playing with her.

This was perfectly in accordance with my own excited feelings, and I threw myself into her arms at once, how she kissed me all over, then stretching her body over me, with her head towards my feet, buried her face between my thighs, and sucked me so deliciously, that I could not help doing the same to her, making her fairly emit her love juice into my mouth over and over again, whilst she for her part sucked every atom of honey that was to be extracted from my little virgin flower.

What a night that was, but at last tired out by the excess of our lubricity, we sank into a refreshing sleep, and only awoke long after daylight, by the children in the nursery calling out for Phoebe.

"Run back and make some excuse, my dear," exclaimed Miss Wilberforce, almost pushing me off the bed, "but mind not a word to any one, and Mr. Royston shall come here this evening to hear your explanation, but don't be frightened, I won't let him hurt you."

In the course of the day Miss Mabel whispered to me that Mr. Royston had determined to give me a whipping for my spying, but it should not be too severe? and that she was going to give the other servants and children something to make them sleep well, in case of any noise.

What a trepidation the announcement put me into, the very idea of being punished by a great strong man like the farmer seemed awful. He must have a heavy hand I thought.

I dreaded the night, which seemed to come only too soon, I couldn't look at Mr. Royston, or meet his eye in any way, and was conscious of being continually on the blush as I waited at table.

Miss Wilberforce ordered me to come to her room in my nightdress, as soon as the children were fast asleep.

I was put into her bed, whilst she, having undressed, sat down in a dressing gown to read the little book I had seen the night before.

Presently coming to the bed, she sat down on the side, and said, "Look here, Phoebe dear, that is what you will have to bear."

I turned my eyes to the book, and saw a picture of a naked man whipping a little girl with a birch rod, the culprit seemed to be crying out with tears in her eyes, whilst a lady also naked was kneeling down and caressing, the stiffened engine of bliss which stuck out in front of the gentleman.

"Do you know, Phoebe," she went on, "that birching is a great inducement to the pleasures of love, and excites both ladies and gentlemen so much that it is often indulged in, not for the purposes of punishment, but to increase their enjoyment, so you need not fear it is so very dreadful; see, here are several more plates showing how the act of love is done, you are too young for that yet, but shall see us do it, and mind, you make yourself useful, Mr. Royston wants you to handle that great thing of his, and after playing with it a little you must insist upon helping him to put it into me, and tickle him behind whilst he is having his fun."

"Have you got little Phoebe here?" asked Mr. R— entering the room in his shirt at the moment.

"Here she is, dear, in my bed," replied Miss Mabel, "but don't be too severe with her."

"You little minx!" he said, approaching the bed, "I've got a bumttckler for you, at least I told Miss Wilberforce to make one; I'll teach you to peep at me again!"

"Oh, pray sir, oh — I don't know what made me do it," I said, frightened, and beginning to sob.

"Out you come, Phoebe! It's no use snivelling before you're touched. Miss Mabel shall whip you well, till you promise never to peep again," he said sharply.

Afraid of the consequences, I tremblingly obeyed, and stood with tearful eyes before Miss Wilberforce. "Oh, do sir, forgive me this once," I sobbed.

"No, no, no, you've seen too much, we must make sure of her silence. Mabel, dear, make her kneel down in front of me, as I sit in the easy chair, then I can hold her head and shoulders, whilst you can tackle her bum properly for her," he said, then seating himself I had to kneel in front of him as if saying my prayers, whilst he pulled up my night-dress over my head, and pressed me down right over his organ of love, which I could feel sticking up under his shirt, and throbbing against my face.

They didn't give me much time to think about my position. Swish went the rod, and I felt a sharp stinging cut right round my naked posteriors. Another and another followed in rapid succession. Swish — swish — swish, etc., and if I had not stuffed my night-dress into my mouth, I should have howled with pain, the cuts were so sharp.

"That's right, Mabel, make her feel it till her bottom is well scored with red marks and weals, it's beautiful to see it flush under every cut!" exclaimed Mr., Royston, "touch her upon the tenderest parts, make the ends of the rod tickle the inside of her thighs, don't even let her tittle crack escape free."

He held my head down so tightly, but whether it was my writhing about under the sharp pain, or his own doing I don't know, somehow that great thing of his got uncovered, and was rubbing its nose right in my face.

Remembering Miss Mabel's injunctions, I thought the best plan to avert further punishment would be to fondle it at once, so one hand clasped its immense thickness, whilst my lips caressed the great ruby head; almost in an instant I felt a strong convulsive throb, and if I had not closed my lips at the moment he would have choked me with a tremendous emission, which as it was spurted all over my cheeks and neck.

His hands pressed my face down more and more at the moment, but presently relaxed, and then with a long drawn sigh he leant back exhausted in the chair.

"Look now, you rude girl, what have you done to Mr. Royston? Take that — and that —and that — will you ever peep or be so rude again?" The housekeeper almost screamed as she finished me off with three tremendous cuts, which I afterward found had fairly brought the blood, still at the moment I did not feel them so much as I had at 6rst, a warm glow pervaded my veins, and I felt on fire for something inexpressible. The pain and pleasure so intermixed as to excite all the lechery of my youthful nature.

Mr. Royston presently took me on his knee and kissed me for the pleasure he told me I had given him, then asked me a lot of questions about what I had seen on the previous night.

"Why I saw you shove this great thing of yours right into

Miss Wilberforce," I replied, "and it didn't seem to hurt her a bit, and then you both heaved and pushed at one another till you suddenly got tired and almost rolled off her, was it that you spurted something into her, like you did in my face just now, sir?"

I was fondling it with my hands, whilst he repaid me with lots of kisses, as his Angers were playing with and tickling my little slit, so that I could hardly sit on his knee.

Miss Wilberforce had thrown off all her clothes, and was now tossing about naked on the bed.

"Phoebe dear, don't play with that stupid man any longer," she at length burst out. "He must know that great thing of his can't have a little girl, bring him here at once to me, darling, or he will again shoot his love juice, and waste what I ought to have."

He had just thrust his tongue in my mouth, but I wrenched my face away, and springing from his lips drew him to the bed by his Cupid's battering ram, then as he got over his longing lady love I slapped his bottom as hard as I could with one hand, whilst the other directed Mr. John Thomas into the haven of bliss, and continued to tickle his hirsute appendages as they dangled against her beautiful buttocks at every plunge.

He seemed rather lazy over the business, but she, to judge by the way she clasped her arms round his neck, threw her legs over his loins, and heaved up to meet every shove of his great engine, (which I could see was glistening with the nectar of love, she could not retain directly he was into her), was in a perfect rage of lustful desire.

"Get the rod, Phoebe," she exclaimed, "and pay him out for whipping you, he is not half brisk enough for me, and will be all night coming if you don't make his bum smart, my dear!"

Too pleased not to do it, I snatched up the rod, and did my duty so well that his posteriors were soon wealed and scored, till they began to look quite raw, and he fairly bounded under my strokes.

At last they came together with cries of delight, such as "you love, you dear, oh shove it into me — give me all — every inch.

Ah —oh, oh, oh! I shall die! etc," from Miss Mabel, whilst Mr. Royston audibly groaned out, "Oh, heavens! My God! What a delightful spend!" and then both of them seemed perfectly exhausted for a few minutes as they lay listlessly in each others arms, with their eyes shut, and their limbs loosely but lightly intertwined.

After this I stayed with them rather over a year, and during that time assisted at many of their little parties of pleasure.

At length Mr. Royston, who was really very fond of me, thought I ought to learn a business, so they brought me to town, and apprenticed me to Madame Coulisse, a fashionable milliner, who occupied the whole of the upper part of a large house in New Bond Street.

She had six young ladies as assistants, besides myself and three others as apprentices or improvers, as well as Miss Wallis, the cutter out and sub-manageress under herself.

Our hours were tolerably easy, in fact much more so than I had expected, after all the tales I had heard about overwork, etc. We were only kept to business from nine a.m. to six p.m. daily, in fact there never seemed a great abundance of work about, a few ladies certainly came every day upon business, but Madame evidently did not give great satisfaction, as I heard them complain of the work, and customers very seldom seemed to favour her with a second order.

The apprentices were sent to bed about eight o'clock, and we often heard loud laughing as if gentlemen were in the house, and a great deal of running up and down stairs.

Madame seemed very fond of me, and I was treated with great kindness, in fact she soon had me to act as a lady's maid to herself, and being often alone with her she got from me the complete tale of my previous life.

"*Ma foi*," she exclaimed, when I had told her all, for she regularly wormed it all from me, "but you are von leetle cocotte, I will soon make you grand lady. Phoebe is too common a name for my house, I will call you Vanessa, from Milord Byron — good name make fortune."

Then she explained to me that her millinery business was all a sham to keep the house respectable, and that every evening gentlemen came to see the young ladies. "You have gentlemans, and I give you Ane clothes, and no nothing to do."

So the bargain was concluded as it were without my even saying a word.

CHAPTER II

Sale of my Virginity to a Gentleman,
who takes me away from the the House in New Bond Street.

IT TOOK A DAY OR TWO FOR MADAME COULISSE
to rig me out with all new clothes. She actually sent me to another milliner to have my things
made in the best possible fashion, then one Sunday afternoon she took me and two of her young ladies for a drive in Hyde Park, during which I noticed several gentlemen stop and speak to her in a lew tone, as they looked at me rather significantly. This was her market. I was sold to advantage before we drove back to the house.

The same evening, about ten o'clock. MadLune sent for me to her boudoir, she had previously told me to make myself look my very best, as she expected to be able to introduce me to a very nice gentleman during the evening (of course keeping to herself the fact of having sold my maidenhead for a couple of hundred pounds).

On entering I saw a fine aristocratic-looking man seated by her side on a sofa.

"Allow me, Milord, to introduce Mdlle. Vanessa. Have you ever seen a prettier little thing, she is barely thirteen, and I warrant her genuine." Then turning to me, "This gentleman, Vanessa, wishes to honour you with his love, be as good a girl as you promised, my dear, and you will have nothing but happiness to look forward to in my house," saying which she vanished from the room, and left me *vis-a-vis* with his lordship, who rose, kissed my lips, and drew me to his side on the sofa.

"So my little dear you are willing to make love with me, look, if I am pleased I shall give you these sovereigns," showing me a handful of gold. "When I make love I don't like crying and sulks, it takes it all out of me."

I blushed awfully, but when he kissed me again I gave him a little one in return, as I clung round his neck, and promised to try and please him if he would not hurt me much.

"Ah, then you know a little, my dear?"

"Yes, madame has told me it hurts first, and gives great delight afterwards — I — I want to be a woman, sir!"

"And so you shall, let us undress, and try what yonder spring bed will do for us, by Jove! I'll take you and keep you if you please me, Vanessa, I want a girl no one has ever had."

We were both soon reduced to a state of complete nudity, except stockings and garters, then lifting me on the bed he jumped up beside me, and began to examine all my charms, first my firm round little bubbies, then my mount just sprouting as it was with a light silky growth of hair, but the spot below was too attractive for him to linger long before he put his 6nger there.

It made me wince, the passage was too narrow and tender.

"You love!" he exclaimed, Ms eyes almost darting 6re as he spoke, whilst I actually saw his manly affair quite suddenly lift its head, which had up to this been only partially erected. "You love! you're a real virgin, are you not? How I shall love you, Vanessa! Now? be good, and bear a little pain for the sake of the pleasure to come, then I will pay the old bitch her money, and take you away. I won't leave such a jewel in her care for a moment, she would sell you again before to-morrow night. No, darling, you must belong to me alone!"

Then raising my buttocks, he put a pillow under my bottom, and getting between my legs, his fingers gently opened the lips of my pussey, and pointing the head of his moderate-sized dart of love to the entrance, he pushed as far as it would go, then feeling the obstruction of my hymen, he paused for a moment, then thrust so suddenly and fiercely that I fainted from the excessive pain, but he effected his purpose at once, so that my defloweration was complete, and he was buried to the roots of his hair when I came to myself in a minute or two.

Presently he began to move, thrusting slowly in and out, with a poking kind of motion, then I felt his warm juice spurt right up into my vitals as it were, and so oil the wounded passage that I soon began to feel some pleasureable sensations, which increased as he went on again till I began to meet him with all the ardour of my warm temperament, now fairly aroused for the first time to the true joys of womanhood.

How we struggled, lovingly and yet almost furiously, to get more love from each other. My champion was a good man, and his size just suited me, we swam in delight three times before he was compelled to cry a go.

Then embracing me most tenderly, he sponged my lacerated parts till he had cooled them, and removed all trace of the havoc he had committed. I really loved him for his tender kindness, and when he made me dress and took me in his carriage, in spite of all Madame's protestations that she would not have me taken away, I threw my arms round his neck and sobbed with tears of gratitude.

We went to a fine hotel, and the next day saw me installed as his mistress in a pretty suite of chambers at the West End, near Belgrave Square.

I do not want to mention his name, but shall simply call him My Lord, he was so kind to me, and I believe from the first almost loved me to distraction, he got French, English, and musical governesses for me, and took the greatest possible pleasure in seeing me do the honours of his table when a friend or friends visited at our chambers, but it was not to last long, only two brief happy, happy years, and then all was blown to the winds, at least of that real and pure happiness which I enjoyed with him.

He had a bosom friend, a Mr. Gower, in fact a regular chum, who spent hours with him every day, they were partners in every sport, on turf and in everything. He was a much younger and handsomer man than his lordship, and being so often in his company, sometimes he would call and catch me alone, and wait for my protector.

My God! what an oily tongue that serpent had! How he flattered me and led me on till I really loved him as much as his friend, it was rank adultery. I felt I must have him, and that he would soon ask me to be unfaithful to my protector, to whom I owed my happiness, my all; still I knew I should yield, I had a fancy and couldn't help myself.

At last the fatal promise was given, but we had to wait for an opportunity for the feast of love we were to taste on the sly.

Our's were the only inhabited chambers in the house at night, and his lordship seldom left me to sleep alone.

At last the chance came, my protector had a great match on at Newmarket, but Mr. Gower was too ill to go with him. As soon as he had started I gave my servant a holiday for the night, and about eight o'clock in the evening my paramour came. I was careful to put up the chain to the street door, his lordship had a latch key, and my guilty conscience told me there was just a chance of his return, although extremely improbable.

How lovingly we walked up the stairs together, after a long luscious kiss behind the street door. I had prepared a nice little cold collation with plenty of champagne, for I must admit having always had a great partiality for the sparkling fizz.

How he bore me to the sofa in a perfect transport of impatience, raised my clothes, and kneeling down, printed hot burning kisses on the sensitive spot itself, till I fairly begged he would give me a better proof of his manhood.

Our first conjunction was far too impassioned to last long, we came together at once in a Hood of bliss, but he kept his place, and soon almost drove me out of my mind by the thrilling effect of his thrusts, he was a little bigger made than his lordship, and Riled me up so tightly that it seemed most exquisite. However, this second turn came to the usual delicious ending, then we sat down to supper, and I must confess he was allowed to pledge me so frequently in bumpers of champagne, that I got quite lecherous, threw off my clothes, made him undress, and then persisted in sitting on his lap with his fine John Thomas buried to the hilt in my crack, and throbbing inside in response to the delicious love grips my tight sheath kept indulging him with.

At last we went to bed, and then commenced a regular battle of love, my champion was quite my equal in lust; how we joined and grappled in our love struggles, each one unable to subdue the raging fires of the other, or even a little quench the constantly increasing flame of desire.

"Hark! I hear a key in the street door," I whispered in alarm, "it must be My Lord returned, what shall we do?"

The craven-hearted coward was frightened in a moment, and would have been caught where he was but I had the presence of mind to shove him into a closet on the landing, and throw his clothes after him. The bell was ringing furiously, and the knocker made a fearful din. So kicking all the debris of the supper under the table, and only leaving my own plate and glass, I at last put on a wrapper and let him in.

"What a time you were, Vanessa, there's been an accident on the line, so I returned to town, and shall go in the morning again."

"Yes, love, I couldn't help it, I was fast asleep, the fact is I've drunk a whole bottle of fizz to myself, dearie," I replied with a feigned yawn.

"Zounds, girl! what a state the bed is in!" he exclaimed, noticing it for the first time. "Who have you had here?"

"No one, love, pray don't look so cross, I have been tossing about for hours thinking of you, and only a little while ago fell off to sleep and had a frightful night-mare, dreaming we had been captured by brigands, they tied you to a tree, and were just drawing lots who was to have your little girl, when your knocking and ringing put an end to it; wouldn't it have been awful to have been really true?"

"Then I suppose, Vanessa, that I'm the brigand to have you, now I've got in?" he said, his face relaxing into a smile, and beginning to throw off his clothes. "I wanted you awfully a little while ago, when our train was blocked on the line and that is the cause of my coming back for a bit of love."

"Then love, come to bed quickly, I do want you so, you will divert my thoughts, and cool my hot blood," I said, hoping to distract his attention, and prevent notice being taken of the debris under the table, and more especially as I fancied I heard my gallant sneaking downstairs at the moment.

Throwing off his clothes, he carried me to the bed with an impetuosity quite unusual to him, as he laid me upon my back and got between my readily opening legs, my hand guided his impatient courser to the love mark, which, notwithstanding all its previous battering and the right I had had, was again in a tremor of longing expectation, my blood had been so fired by the champagne that my lubricity was perfectly unquenchable, I felt as if I could have engaged a dozen lusty men, one after the other, at that moment.

The insertion of a second priapus in my excited affair seemed such a *bon bouche* and unexpected pleasure, as it glided slowly up the well-lubricated sheath, and if he had not been especially amorous he must have noticed that I was not nearly so tight as usual on a first penetration. My arms clasped him closely to my body, our lips met in hot burning kisses, I sucked his tongue into my mouth in the most lascivious manner, my legs crossing over his buttocks with all the abandon of a perfect bacchante.

Almost in an instant, before he had given more than three

vigorous thrusts, I felt the warm rush of his seed up into my very vitals, which had such a thrilling effect on me that my own emission instantly flowed in response to his, the floodgates of love mingled their flow in the most extatic manner.

Without for a moment relaxing in stiffness, his weapon kept its place in my hot throbbing sheath, and soon commenced another course (it must have been the heat of my vagina, which infused, or rather, kept such strength in him, for it was quite unusual), his swollen and eager courser plunged forward in the most vigorous manner, and so worked up all the lubricity of my! nature, that quite forgetting everything else, I fancied it was my paramour still in my arms, and just at the moment of coming, I murmured "Oh, Henry! Oh, Gower, I shall die, you kill me with love you darling."

He sprang from my embrace as if a serpent had stung him, exclaiming, "Vile wretch, that's it, is it, he must have been here when I came? Ha! what's this, his watch, by God!" as he caught a glimpse of the chain peeping from under the pillow, and thrusting his hand under brought out the damning evidence of our guilt.

"Revenge is sweet, however," he went on, grinding his teeth and white with rage, "I'll kill you first and him afterwards."

Paralyzed with fear, and seeing him take up a small stiletto belonging to myself, from the toilet table, I threw myself on my knees, all naked as I was, and clasped my hands round his waist, imploring and shrieking for mercy! mercy! ! mercy! ! ! mercy! ! ! afraid to look up and meet his relentless look. My face was buried in the dark hair at the bottom of his belly, with his stiff pego brushing against my cheek in undiminished size, as if also as indignant as its owner.

"Too late, Vanessa, you should have thought of that before, nothing but blood can wipe out such injuries!" he hissed rather than spoke, at the same time I felt one arm grasped by his powerful hand, wrenching me away from his body, and a perfect rain of stabs pierced neck, bosom, and arms. Shrieking I bit his arm in my struggle for life, and as he let go slipped under the bed for protection from him, where, covered with blood, I sobbed and begged to be spared, promising never even to mention it or prosecute him, if he would but fetch a doctor to save me from bleeding to death.

Strange to say, he now relented, and ran for a surgeon. "Save her life, save me from being her murderer, and keep our secret, here's £500 and a 1000 more if you cure her!" he said nervously, as he brought Dr. Smithson to the side of my bed, where I was weltering in my blood.

As for myself I had crawled upon the bed, and wrapped the sheets as tightly as possible round my wounds, instinctively feeling they were not mortal, unless the How of blood should be too great.

"My lord, you may rely upon my honour as a gentleman, unless the case proves fatal," was the reply. "I will do my best You had better not have a nurse, I will attend to the case myself, and get some one to mind my patients meanwhile; I do not think it will be more than a fortnight before she is convalescent, and if I act as nurse the secret will be safe," said the doctor when he had dressed my wounds.

There is no occasion to go into the details of my recovery, his lordship never saw me again, and in about a month's time the doctor handed me a cheque for £2000, saying he thought I should now be able to shift for myself.

CHAPTER III

Travels and Adventures. In Search of Renewed Health.
Return to London, and Take a House.

BY DR. SMITHSON'S ADVICE I DETERMINED TO
go to Naples for a few months, so in a few days I found a
ladylike person, about thirty-five, who undertook to be my
chaperone for a salary of £10 per month, and all expenses paid.

Mademoiselle Zara de Foutre seemed to me a highly
accomplished and desirable companion, speaking French,
German, and Italian fluently, so having invested the sum of
£1500 in Consols, and provided myself with necessary letters of
credit, we sailed from London in the steamer Garonne, for the
capital of what used to be called the Two Sicilies.

I hardly got over my sea-sickness before we came in sight of
Gibraltar, but the short stay for the necessary operation of coaling
only admitted of a very short stay on shore. However, I now
began to feel much stronger, and under the influence of sunny
skies and delightful sea breezes, I began to feel the necessity of
a voluptuous adventure such as would accord with the natural
warmth of my constitution, and satisfy the craving of my sensual
appetites.

We had a lot of handsome young fellows on board, on their
way to India, many of whom in the course of their harmless
flirtations caused the flame of desire to thrill through my veins,
but however pleasant these utterings of emotion might be, there
was no chance of being able to enjoy anything more, as they were
all two or four in a little cabin, and we also had two young ladies
in the same compartment with myself and chaperone.

Captain Beard, the commander of the vessel, was a regular

lady's man, and had been so very kind in his enquiries about me, during the first few distressing days of the voyage, and I now noticed he eyed my every movement, and as I knew he had a spacious cabin all to himself, as well as being a handsome middle aged man, exactly the sort of fellow who can please a thoroughly lecherous girl, as I only too well knew myself to be (a man of the world not too much used up, is far better than any youthful lover, the latter is too impetuous to satisfy, whilst the former draws out his pleasure to such lengths, and knows so many delightful devices for raising desire and increasing excitement, that they make the women love them in spite of themselves).

I gave him every possible encouragement, and if eyes can speak, plainly told him what I wanted.

When not on duty he continually attached himself to me, played draughts with me, or brought out books for me to read, amongst others, "Moths by Ouida."

The evening after leaving Gibraltar I was reading on deck, till just as it was getting dusk I found him by my side.

"Well, Miss De Vere, (that was the name I had assumed), what is your opinion of Ouida as an authoress?"

"Ah, Captain Beard, you must be a naughty man to give me such a book to read, there is very little left to tell, and that can be imagined!" I replied.

"I'm sure it's a highly proper book."

"Then, sir, I'm sure you have worse in your cabin library, how I should like to have a rummage there when it is your watch on deck," I said laughingly.

"Hem! so that's your opinion, is it, Miss De Vere; well, I will tell you in confidence that I have a really naughty book, called "Fanny Hill," which an old maiden lady, I once had for a passenger, left behind in her cabin, and the stewardess brought it to me; of course, I told Mrs. Robins that I should burn it, but it was too good to be destroyed."

"For shame, sir! Mind no one hears you telling me, but you really have excited my curiosity captain, and you know nothing is scandalous unless found out," I said, archly. "Now, couldn't you lend me that book to read? Sub Rosa, of course!"

"Why!" he ejaculated, with a laugh, "I can lend you 'Sub Rosa' itself, it is a magazine, but only the first three numbers have come out yet, there is a hitch of some sort about the publication, you know that sort of thing often gets seized by he police in England, it is rather free and funny, but nothing compared to 'The Pearl'."

" 'The Pearl,' what's that, a book?"

"Yes, the most extraordinary magazine ever brought out in parts, I have it complete for the eighteen months it came out, plates and all, but it's too bad for a young lady to look at."

"What a naughty man you are to mention things, and say I mustn't see them, but I must sir! I'm not afraid, and can take care of myself, still, captain, dear, I might perhaps go as far as a kiss, if you promise to behave yourself; now will you let me see them?"

"Yes, dear Miss De Vere, if you can guess that riddle, you can read it by the binnacle lamp, but I know you won't be able to answer it."

He gave me a slip of paper, which I took to the light, and read as follows:

A RIDDLE.

Letitia has a large one, and so has cousin Luce, Eliza has a small one, though large enough for use;
A child may have a little one enclosed within a clout;
In fact, all females have one, no girl is born without;
But men, nor boys, nor bucks, nor bear, nor ram, was ever known; To have one either large or small,
to rightly call his own;
All fowls have one — not cocks, of course;
and though prolific breeders, The fact that fish have none is known to piscatorial readers.

Hermaphrodites have none, mermaids are minus too,
Nell Gwynne possessed a double share, we read,
if books are true.
Lasciviousness there has its source, harlots their use apply,
Without it lust had never been, and even love would die.
'Tis used by all in nuptial bliss, in carnal pleasure found,
Destroy it life becomes extinct, the world has but a sound.
Beneath a soft and glossy curl, each lass has one in front, To
find it on an animal, you at the stem must hunt.
Now tell me what the object is? but pause before you guess it,
If you are mother, maid, or man, I swear you don't possess it!

"You impudent man, to give me such a thing as that to guess
at, of course it's too bad to mention!" I said, running back to
where he sat.

"Ha! ha! he laughed." It is quite harmless, and as innocent as
possible, of course every-body thinks its something dirty, but
can't you see it's only the letter L—?"

"But you won't deprive me of the sight of your curiosities of
literature, because I couldn't guess that seemingly rude riddle?"

"You are such a dear young lady, I haven't the heart to refuse,
but you know it's awfully imprudent, even with an old fellow
like me, who has to set a good example to all the passengers and
crew, why if they once thought me even the slightest bit immoral
I should have to give up the ship, it would not be thought safe
for single ladies or young wives, without their husbands to go in
my vessel. Luckily, we have no gamblers on board, (they often sit
up all night, and spoil every chance of even an innocent lark),
after eleven o'clock there won't be a soul stirring, you can then
slip into my cabin, and look at the books and pictures I will leave
on the table, my watch isn't up till twelve, then I can join you
and explain anything you might like to know. Dear Miss De
Vere, you have made my heart all of a flutter, only to think of the
kiss you promise, I must leave you till then, or they may say I'm
having a flirtation with you, au revoir!"

On plea of a headache I kept on deck, and did not retire at the same time as Mdlle. Zara and the other two young ladies who occupied our cabin, and as soon as I found all clear, slipped into the captain's room, which was a most comfortably furnished place, roomy, with a good sized table under a brilliant swinging lamp at one side, whilst at the other was his berth with the curtains closely drawn. Several small books, with very unpretending covers, lay upon the table, and at once attracted my attention, so I sat down for a good look over them. The first I took up had a curious frontispiece of a gentleman holding his cocked hat partly in front of a laughing face, whilst his open breeches exposed the delight of life in all its rampant glory; an extraordinary thrill passed through my whole frame as I caught sight of it, and caused me to exclaim to myself almost *sotto voce*, "How I should like to see the real thing at this moment!"

"You have your wish, darling!" some one said in reply, which gave me quite a start, as I thought it must be one of the young officers or a passenger, but to my great astonishment there was the captain getting out of his berth, and nothing but his shirt to cover his nakedness. "What a fairy you must be, Miss De Vere, you wished, and, Presto! here it is, all alive and real!" as he raised his shirt to expose a fine looking ladies' toy to my astonished gaze.

"Pray, sir, for heaven's sake! cover up that awfully dreadful looking thing!" I said in a loud whisper.

"It's only that to an old maid, not to a delightfully voluptuous minded pretty girl as I guess you to be. Darling, you can't look me in the face and say truthfully that you are a stranger to the delights of sexual intercourse?"

"No, captain, I don't wish to pretend to such squeamish morality, according to my code of morals; love is very nice, and a proper thing to indulge in between discreet people, and is only immoral and scandalous when found out. I would never have encouraged you, as I know I have, had I not believed you to be a very prudent man with a reputation to preserve."

"Your remarks show more wisdom than I should have expected in one so young; besides, do you not find that we middle aged men of the world know better how to please the ladies, and prolong the pleasure than young men or youths who are so impetuous that everything is over almost before you begin to realise its pleasures. This is 'Fanny Hill,' the celebrated book that everybody has heard of, but so few seen, because it is so difficult to purchase, as shopkeepers who risk selling such books are liable to two years imprisonment," he said, taking a book from the table and drawing me on his lap on the couch, at the end of the cabin, where I sat on his knee as he turned over the leaves, and pointed out all the variety of enjoyment depicted in the numerous and luscious plates.

My whole frame quivered with emotion, and I could feel his frightfully stiff affair throbbing under my bottom as I sat on his lap, and hardly resisted his busy hands, as they were rapidly unfastening every part of my dress.

My head dropped on his shoulder as I whispered faintly, "Oh, do let me go, it is too bad to have let me see such things!" Yet I never made any effort to get away from him; he glued his lips to mine, and tipped the velvet so delightfully that my tongue involuntarily responded to the loving challenge, and at the same moment a blissful shudder, which ran through my body, must have let him know that the critical moment had arrived in spite of myself.

"My God, darling, I have made you come!" he said, laying me gently back on the sofa, "I must kiss you till you come again, and suck up every drop of the pearly nectar of love as it distils from the petals of your rosebud."

Almost quicker than I can write it he had turned up my skirts and found the critical spot, my legs opened mechanically at the first touch of his lascivious tongue, as I felt it at the entrance of my crack.

Good heavens! how he tickled my clitoris, as I came again and again, my very soul seemed to melt into his mouth, under the combined titillation of his tongue, fingers and long beard, which last, by its friction on the lips of my slit, added considerably to my exquisite pleasure.

At last I begged he would get up and let me have him in the orthodox fashion, but he first divested himself of his shirt, then pulled off everything from me till I was as naked as he was, then throwing himself upon me, his mouth sought not my lips, but the little strawberry nipples of my small firm orbs of love. The ravenous manner in which he sucked and almost devoured them was so exciting that I threw my legs over his buttocks, and with my right hand took hold of his modest affair which had been resting and palpitating on my belly, as if afraid to go near my Venus's wrinkle.

How I burned to feel it inside me, his ardent attentions to my titties shot such a flame of desire to the very tips of my toes that it was impossible to delay any longer. My hand placed the head to my slit, and a slight upward heave of my bottom sheathed it to the hilt at once, as he was not big, and my plentiful emissions had so lubricated the passage.

Both of us seemed driven into a lustful fury by the previous long and loving dalliance, the Rood gates were opened, and my copious emission so delighted him that I was quite afraid his cries of extasy would be heard by someone.

"You darling, you love! How delicious, you make me come in a moment! My God! there it is! For heaven's sake do something to me — pinch me — put your hand on me. Ah ah! Ah! ! I'm done for, love" as he almost fainted.

After this we had some champagne, then producing a light switch of birch, nothing would please Mm but I must whip his bottom with it, even though I made the skin look quite raw and scratched all over. It both amused and excited me, and I was amply repaid for my trouble, by the increased ardour this essence of birch seemed to instil into him.

It was nearly daylight before he allowed me to leave, and we repeated our revels the two following nights, and when I went ashore at Malta he insisted upon my taking all I wished for of his erotic collection of books and pictures.

The captain is one of my best friends, and regularly stays at my house every time he is home from a voyage.

I only had one chance of fun at Malta, and that was with a noble young middy, about my own age, who I thought would afford me great pleasure, and accordingly allowed him to take me for a drive, and enjoyed a very considerable amount of *al fresco* love during the excursion.

My next move was to Naples, then to Rome and Florence, and on to France via Genoa and Turin.

At the Holy City I had an adventure with a cardinal at a masked ball, but when we came to the point I found my old lover was actually a eunuch and incapable of sexual intercourse, much as he desired it, in fact it seems that these emasculated beings are madly desirous of coming at women, although they know they must fail at the critical moment. However, my loving toil and submission to his kisses and caresses were well repaid by the presentation of a magniûcent parure of diamonds, as I had indulged the old lecher for several days.

Leaving Lyons by railway for Paris, I dropped in for a laughable adventure. I had three travelling companions, a young dark Indian gentleman, and two Frenchmen, the former who could speak English quite engrossed me to himself, and I was much amused by the remarks of the two natives of France, as they thought I did not understand, and evidently did not care if my blackamoor did.

"Don't you see she's game for it, only he's in the way? What a lascivious eye. Mon dieu! how she makes me stand, when she twists about as she laughs; what a lovely and graceful *Tournure*. Fancy having such an English darling, etc."

All alone with these three (I had sent Mdlle. Zara on to Paris to secure apartments), of course I resolved in my mind whom I liked best.

With returning health my thoughts were getting more

practical and business like. The black though handsome was repulsive to me, on the other hand the two Frenchmen were handsome, vigorous looking fellows, just such as would take a wanton woman's fancy.

My supposed ignorance of French was an advantage I resolved to make the most of.

At every stopping place I had three obsequious cavaliers, the Frenchmen could speak a little English, and pressed me to go with them to the Grand Hotel at Paris, and they would pay all expenses, assuring me they were independent gentlemen, which on arrival at the South Eastern terminus I agreed to do, declining a similar invitation from the Indian, and wishing him "Au revoir" just to air my little French.

At the table d'hote, and in the evening to the theatre, my new friends were all compliments, and little double entendres in broken English, and when I finally parted with them for the night it was with great hopes of seducing me on their side, which I had carefully fanned all the while they were with me.

Bolting the door carefully, as I fancied they might be bold enough to take the liberty of intruding on my privacy, I proceeded to undress and have a bath, which I had ordered to be prepared in the room. Once or twice I fancied I heard a suppressed sigh or some one breathing in the room, and thought that whoever they were, the sight would do them good, and it tickled my fancy to think what a rampagious state the sight of my naked figure might drive them into.

A deeper sigh than usual drew my attention to the bed, certainly there was a person in it, and moving too. Quick as thought and naked as I was, I rushed across the room, and pulling off the bedclothes, there lay my Indian in the very act of emission, I had caught him with his hands upon himself, enjoying the sight of my bathing and his masturbation at the same time.

"Dear lady, forgive me, your charms made me desperate and when you preferred those two *canaille* of Frenchmen to me, an Indian prince, I resolved to have you in spite of all. I can do anything here, as I pay for my rooms in the hotel all the year round. Jump into bed as you are, don't put on your envious night chemise!"

"Not with a black man, no money shall tempt me; be off, or I'll ring for help!" I exclaimed.

"Every woman has her price, and yours shall be diamonds," he laughed. "See, I will place this necklet around my standing Priapus, and your own hand must remove it; and then anything else you may wish for shall be yours."

Too good to be refused and resolved to make the most of such a Croesus, I got into bed by his side, and taking my handkerchief wiped and kissed his affair as I took possession of the guerdon of love, then kneeling over his face I presented my longing gap to his lips for him to kiss, and shall never forget how he sucked and thrust in his tongue, it was the longest I ever knew a man to have, the warm bath had so warmed and prepared me for pleasurable excitement, that I fell back in extasy almost in a moment after feeling the lascivious touches of that electric tongue, this made him furious with lust, he sprang up and threw himself upon me with all the impetuosity of his nature. His love dart entered, it filled and continued to swell up inside my vagina in such an extraordinary manner, that I had never felt anything like it before. If his arms had not encircled me like a vice, I could not have got away from him, he could neither push further or withdraw. He kissed me, and thrust his tongue into my mouth, till I could scarcely get my breath, while both our bodies trembled with emotion, and I could feel a constantly recurring emission from him every few minutes.

How long this lasted it is impossible to say, for I fainted, and when I came to myself should have been sure it was only some frightful nightmare, but for the casket and diamond necklet, besides a rouleau of notes which I found on the dressing-table.

At dejeuner I was joined by my two Frenchmen, and heard one tell the other that the only way to get me was to make me drunk, so they invited me to take wine in their apartments, but they little reckoned they would meet their match, as I slyly emptied every glass under the table, and joining them in every toast, at last had the satisfaction of seeing both of them under the table, where I left my lovers who had got through one hundred and fifty francs worth of wine to no purpose.

The night I spent with my Indian prince, and experienced the same delightfully awful sensations, and again met my Frenchmen at dejeuner in the morning. One now plainly told the other that money was my object, observing, "give her one thousand francs of our notes," with a sly laugh, which made me at once suspect they were escrocs or card sharpers. After the repast one of them escorted me to the drawing room, and finding ourselves alone, threw himself on a sofa by my side, and coolly taking out his John Thomas in a standing state, told me it was the yesterday's champagne had so heated him he must have me.

"What a joke, Monsieur, but perhaps I might for the one thousand francs your friend told you to offer me; that is, if they are genuine!" I replied laughingly in French.

"*Ma foi*, and you understood all we have talked about, but look, my notes are genuine!" as he handed me a five hundred franc note; "Look, I have more like it as soon as I've enjoyed you," he said, holding the case open for me to put it back with its companions; but instead of doing so I abstracted another, which I saw in a moment was a flash one.

"Ha! that's how you would serve me, is it, you cheat; begone this instant, or I will inform the hotel people of your character. Go quietly and I shall only retain the genuine five hundred francs to pay my hotel bill. But for decency's sake put away that shame-faced affair of yours; see his drooping head, you might walk out with it proudly, but like that no woman would see it without disgust."

That was the end of them, they sneaked away from the hotel without settling their bill, but my Indian Nabob paid it for them, and kept so close to me during my stay in Paris that I didn't have a chance of another adventure. He wanted me, as a travelling companion, but being enriched to the extent of over £60,000 and my jewellery, I thought of returning to London and persuaded him to take Mdlle. Zara, having first made a bargain with that mercenary young lady to share all profits as long as he kept her, which has brought me in quite £5,000 a year ever since.

In spite of all my good fortune my aversion to the tyranny of a husband, and my naturally wanton nature impelled me to continue a gay life.

On the journey to London I picked up a handsome officer of the Guards, who, when we started from Dover, secured a first class compartment to ourselves in the mail express to Victoria, and compensated himself by a good old-fashioned English f—k on the seat of our carriage, declaring the French whores were damnable in comparison to a modest English girl, which I passed myself off for. I pleased him so, and allowed him to kiss everything, and so cast my glamoured spell around him, that ere we reached town I had the promise of an establishment at Kenningston to be furnished at his expense, while we stayed at the Grand Hotel. In a week it was ready, and I took up my abode here, but my guardsman was too hot even for my wanton constitution, there was hardly a bed, table, couch, or chair but he would have me upon it; go where he would the f——g mania was upon him, especially if he saw a fresh piece of furniture to have me upon. Pianos were his especial delight, to mount my posteriors up on the keys, and either suck or f—k me in that position, was the greatest pleasure he could have; in fact, it was a standing joke amongst the officers of his corps about "pianos getting out of time so soon, where Capt. Somerville had his strum upon them."

Besides this he was so awfully jealous my life began to be miserable, so that at last when one day, furiously complaining of my flirtation, he asked me if I was tired of him. "Yes, certainly," I replied, "and the sooner you give me up the better!"

His feelings were so hurt that he instantly wrote me a cheque for £1,000, and told me I might keep the house and shift for myself. This exactly suited the plans I had been marking out for myself as soon as I could get quit of him, without apparently acting with palpable ingratitude, You are too well acquainted with the doings in my house for me to give an account of my present life, but should you wish for a Christmas party next year, and you are a good boy in the meantime, I may look up and jot down for your amusement some of the voluptuous adventures which I have heard of, or been a party to, since I became such a well known member of the Demi-Monde.

For the present this is the end of Vanessa.

Everyone complimented Spencer on his tale, and then their host turning to Fuckatilla, said, "You know, my little dear, the treat I promised you; I think Vanessa's story has warmed me up for the business of five to one, there are only four males in the party, but I have a nice dildoe for your cousin, and when Emma straps it on she will be as good as a man, and last a deal longer. We will all have a sip of my magic Mouche D'Espagne chocolate, which I have kept in reserve on the hob, to invigorate us for the last orgie of the night, then to work."

The tiny cups were handed round, and even little Nelly had hers to sip; the effect was indeed magical, each prick in a few moments stood in a state of bursting grandeur, the girls' eyes Rushed with lustful desires. Nelly was down on her knees, almost devouring Jack Turdey's affair, so ravenously did she gamahuche him, as she begged that as he had a moderate sized cock he would try and make a real woman of her.

"No, no, my little darling!" said Bigcock, as he excitedly fastened the dildoe on Cousin Emma, an enormous thing, about nine inches long, and thick in proportion. "You shall work off your excitement by birching us all round, as there is nothing else for you to do. Get that great bunch of birch from the sideboard, and pay us out with it as hard as you can."

A couch without a back was placed in the centre of the room, Cousin Emma reclined on her back, then Fucktilla spitted herself on the dildoe, till her cunt was deliciously gorged by the soft flesh-like india rubber tool which made her spend in a moment, as she bounded on the joy-giving instrument, her cousin sucking her bubbies for her with all the abandon of lust.

Frank Jones and Spencer on either side placed their pricks in her hands to frig, whilst Bigcock presented his for her mouth to suck, and Jack Turdey last of all took the position he so dearly loved *au derriere*, where he revelled in the delightful pleasures of her fundamental rosebud.

Nelly Racquet now applied her rod with vigour, her right hand switching them one by one as she ran round the group, frigging herself with her left hand at the same time, exclaiming every now and then, "Hold tight; go it. Fuck away. You won't let me know what it's like, so I'll pay you all out in spite. Don't your bums look pretty! I've made Jack's bleed." Till at last she was so carried away by the wantonness of her feelings, she dropped the rod, and mounted on Fuckatilla's back, with her bottom to Jack, who had to postillion her with his finger in her tight little arsehole as she screamed with delight.

This scene lasted a long time, each one swimming in lubricity till the effects of the *Mouche D'Espagne* were exhausted.

They had a glass of champagne to revive themselves, then finished the night by all joining in the following:

CHRISTMAS ANTHEM.

Christmas has come! let affection and folly,
Run through the land from the North to the South,
Hang up the mistletoe, nail up the holly,
Frolic and fun be the talk of each mouth,
For each one to flirt, and to drink, and to eat;
Aged and Young, come! now, this is the Season,
All have enjoyment — my prick "sees no reason,"
Why Christmas should pass, and he not have a treat.
Ruddy his tip, as the bright Holly merry!

Round are his balls, as the Pudding so gay;
White pearly drops, like the Mistletoe berry,
They shall distil from his touch-hole to-day.
I will sip toddy, forget worldly scheming.
Prick! I feel for you a friendship sincere;
Pledge me in a draught, and your top ruddy beaming,
Shall quaff the Sweet Cunt Juice, for Christmas is here!
Christmas is here! so my prick, what you fancy,
That you shall have for your holiday fare;
From the black curly jock of the stately Miss Nancy,
To young Kitty's sweet cunt, that can't boast of a hair.
Come! my tail full bosomed fairy of twenty,
Come! little golden haired maiden of eight,
Look round the room, there are partners in plenty,
But nothing like Prick for a Christmas-time Mate!
Let the snow fall — we care not for the weather,
Pile up the logs on the gay crackling Are;
Then shall Queen Cunt and King Prick meet together,
And our sighs of enjoyment in silence expire.
Come! 'tis but once a year — let there be blindness,
To what our warm feelings incline us to do;
Come, merry maidens, and show my Prick kindness,
And straight he will strive to give pleasure to you!
Touch with your hand, let your sweet taper fingers,
Electric-like thrill him from root unto tip;
Then while the warmth of that contact still lingers,
Caress the sweet darling with tongue and with lip.
Press to your bosom — then glide to your Cunny,
Into your belly he'll pour his "good cheer;"
"Will you spend in my bum?" "Should like to, My Honey!"
We will do what we like now, For Christmas is Here!

FINIS.

82